Love Song

SUSAN SCOTT SHELLEY

ACKNOWLEDGMENTS

Thank you to my beta reader/brainstorming team, my clutch group who I can always count on, who I am also lucky to call my friends: Jackie, Beth, Kate, Chantel, and Tina. You guys are the best! Really, I love your brains! Brilliant women, all of you!

Thank you to Scott, my husband and best friend, who creates my beautiful book covers and provides endless inspiration. It's never easy writing through illness and injury, and during the writing of this book, I was felled by both. Your support was the reason I succeeded.

.

CHAPTER ONE

Mind as blank as he could get it, Luke Thompson lounged poolside. The sparkling water and gorgeous day soothed his soul. Not that he deserved soothing. A cloudless sky of brilliant blue met tall green palm trees and the high white stone privacy fence surrounding his band mate Zander's house and yard. Sighing, he rolled onto his back.

Tired. But he could no longer blame that on the tour.

Lonely. But... There wasn't much he could do about that.

To his left, Zander manned the grill. To his right, his other band mates Landry and Brendan wrestled with Zander's dogs on the lawn. Luke closed his eyes and breathed in deep, soaking up the mundane peace. A private oasis. And after months and months of touring and all the drama that had ensued, the quiet seclusion was exactly what he needed.

Laughter drifted along the breeze. He turned his head in time to see Zander step away from the grill to kiss the woman he'd proposed to a month earlier. Jayne was perfect for his best friend, but the way she talked and moved was a constant reminder of the one woman Luke couldn't have—Audrey.

He'd been so fucked up over losing Audrey that he'd nearly ruined Zander and Jayne's relationship. Hell, he'd nearly ruined the band, too. He'd acted like a prick during most of the final leg of the tour, and had jeopardized his relationships with his fans, his label, and most importantly, his band mates. The guys, closer to him than his own family, had been with him for over ten years. Forgiveness had been granted, but he didn't think he could ever make amends for all the drama he'd caused.

He'd sure as hell try, though.

Stretching, he stood. When Jayne caught his gaze, he offered her a smile. Thankfully, she smiled back.

He collected his half-empty beer and wandered closer. "Need a hand with anything?"

"Nope. All done." She set a bowl of salad on a table already laden with enough food to feed their entire road crew.

"Looks great." He turned as Brendan shouted a whoop. Two seconds later, the drummer push Landry into the pool. The bassist should have seen it coming. No way could Brendan resist. Neither could the dogs, who splashed in right after Landry. Not to be outdone, Brendan canonballed into the mix.

Letting out a hollow laugh, Luke sank onto a chair. He should be happy. The tour was over and the summer stretched out before him with promises of long days and nights of freedom. He had a few visits scheduled to audition fans who'd won a contest for a chance to sing with the band, and then the party in Vegas where they'd perform together, but that was it. For the first time in years, he had a vacation. He really *should* be happy.

But inside, all he felt was empty. Deflated. Down. Like a cluster of gray clouds constantly hovered over his head, accompanied by an ache in his soul that wouldn't ease. Broken hearts sucked.

Zander nudged his shoulder. "Steak, fish, or veggie burger?"

He didn't feel like eating but if he didn't choke down something, Jayne would fuss over him. She always went out of her way to take care of the band. "Whatever. Just not veggie."

"Those are mine, anyway." Landry strolled over, dripping wet, and plucked one of the tan circular patties off of the plate by the grill.

Luke forked a piece of steak. Normally, he'd have a smart retort ready to go, but drumming up the energy seemed too much work. Instead, he glanced at Zander. "I thought Irisa was coming."

"Dom is leaving for a road trip today. You know my sister. She's probably spending every second that she can with him before he has to go."

The barking of a dog drew his attention to the house. Irisa, the band's manager and Zander's sister, strolled in tugging a large Great Dane beside her. "Sorry I'm late. I got held up by a phone call."

Jayne hugged her, then laughed as the dog darted straight into the pool. "We figured you got held up by your fiancé."

She smiled a face-splitting grin that shone with the giddy happiness of new-found love. "Well, maybe a bit."

"No worries. The food just came off the grill."

Zander gestured at the table. "Help yourself."

Once they were all seated and eating, Irisa set her fork aside and cleared her throat. "Time to talk business. We have a situation. Vance Dubrow contacted me today."

Everyone groaned in unison, but Luke felt the groan all the way to the pit of his stomach. A direct phone call from the recording label's president was never a good thing.

Zander shook his head and gestured with his beer. "We just got done with the tour. The label knows we're taking a long, overdue, and much needed break. We're doing the fan contest this month, then the fan party in Vegas, and then we're on hiatus. I don't want to hear the words new album, recording, studio sessions, or special performances."

"How about the words *you're done*?"

The words took a second to sink in and then Luke's stomach sank like a lead weight. "What?"

"Are you serious?" Landry formed a fist by his plate. He shot one look at Luke before returning his attention to Irisa.

"Done?" Brendan frowned, his face for once devoid of any smile. "Why?"

Zander reached for Jayne's hand. "What did Vance say?"

"He said that due to all of the drama on the last tour, and album sales not meeting expectations, they've opted to exercise the greatest hits clause in our contract to fulfill the final album obligation. They feel they'll make more money there than spending money on a brand new album from The

Fury. They're releasing it in a month."

Silence reigned. They'd been with the label from the band's inception. Ten years was a long time.

"So, we're free of them? The Fury is no longer part of Excite Records?" Zander carefully looked at his plate, expression unreadable.

Shit. Luke glanced at his band mates. Guilt settled over him like a heavy blanket. Granted, they'd all played a part in things spiraling out of control, but the majority of the blame rested squarely on his shoulders. He'd do whatever they wanted to fix it. "Guys, I'm sorry. We all know I fucked up the most this last tour. I don't want to bring anyone down with me. Maybe the label will reconsider if I'm gone."

Zander's head shook swiftly. "No way, man. We're not losing you."

"We weren't happy with Excite for dicking us around these past few years anyway." Brendan patted his shoulder. "This might be a good thing."

Irisa signaled for their attention. "They've also pulled the plug on the fan contest."

"That's bullshit. It's only six weeks away." Luke slammed his fist on the table. "We created the contest to mend our relationship with the fans. We can't not see that through."

"So what do we do now?" Landry scowled into his beer. "Form our own label?"

Zander snapped his fingers. The light of battle came into his eyes and a slow smile spread across his face. "Hell, yeah. That's exactly what we do. We're forming our own label."

"What are we going to call it—Furious Records?" Brendan laughed and reached for a second burger.

"Actually, I like that name." Luke grinned as the other guys agreed. "How about this? Instead of just winning the chance to perform with us, the fans we select will combine to form a group which will be the first band to sign under our new label. You all know they were hoping for a chance to sign with someone. Might as well be us."

Brendan nodded. "They could open for us on our next tour."

Irisa held up both hands. "Slow down. You're creating a lot of work for me to do. Let me grab something so I can make a list. If we're keeping with the six week timetable, I need to get started now."

Luke pulled out his phone and opened the note app. "My fuck-ups caused most of the drama, so I'll take the lion's share of the work. We need a venue in Vegas, clothes for the new band when we do the unveiling, a name for them, and logos for both our label and them."

Jayne touched his arm. "The fan contest was my idea. I'm happy to help you. We can let the fans choose the new band's name. That would be fun."

"Thanks. We'll also need a press release."

Again, Irisa waved her hand. "Jett Hale called me today. He had a cancellation on his TV show and wanted to know if we could fill in. It would be good for publicity and a great way make this new announcement."

Jett was one of their biggest supporters. They'd

been guests on his New York City based hard rock show numerous times over the years. Luke nodded. "I'm in. When?"

"In about two weeks. Friday, the twelfth."

"Works for me. I have to be in NYC that week anyway for one of my fan auditions." The words came out casually, but Luke felt anything but calm. The city that never sleeps was also the home of the one woman in the world he couldn't forget.

"Lucky you." Brendan frowned into his beer. "I'm in Arizona that week. Do you know how long the flight is from Phoenix to New York?"

Luke glanced at Zander, and then Landry. They all knew how much Brendan hated flying.

Before he could say anything, Landry gave them a slight nod and then threw his wet towel at Brendan's chest. "I'm in Texas then for mine. I'll meet you in Phoenix after that, Bren. We'll travel together."

"Thanks, man. I'm almost sorry I pushed you into the pool now." Brendan grinned, drumming his hands on the table as Landry flipped him off.

The fan auditions were individual—each member auditioning four fans, in four cities, spread out across the country. Luke wouldn't have minded some company in New York. Something to help distract him from Audrey.

As if Irisa read his mind, she cleared her throat. "We need to figure out set design, clothes, and the rest. I know we always use Audrey as our fashion designer. She called me today, before I heard from Vance, to invite me to a fashion show she's hosting on the thirteenth. It's the day after Jett's show, so we'll all be in New York anyway. I'm going to attend. She said to extend the invitation to the band too. I could see if she's available to work with us on this project."

Every head swiveled in Luke's direction. His mouth went dry.

Fuck.

Just hearing her name was enough to slash a fresh blade of regret through his stomach. His fingers clenched the cold bottle in his hand. For the sake of the band, he'd somehow suffer through while the only woman he'd ever dreamed of a forever with would be achingly close and firmly out of reach. "Fine by me."

While the guys compared the rest of their audition dates and flights, he headed into the kitchen under the guise of grabbing more beer for everyone. Anything to work off the nervous energy that filled him. If she agreed to work with them, how the hell would he steel his heart?

Irisa slipped into the room and closed the patio door at her back. "Hey."

He nodded. "Want a beer?"

"Sure," she said casually, but he could tell he'd been cornered alone for a reason. He just hoped to God it wasn't another round of sisterly bullshit.

"About Audrey," she began, taking the microbrew. Her rings glittered in the light shining through the window.

He dragged his gaze from the sparkles to her face. "Yeah?"

"I wasn't sure I should tell you this, but I think Audrey wanted me to tell you, even though she didn't ask me to. She called off the engagement with Dante. They've split."

Hope flared a second before his protective instincts kicked in. If that bastard had hurt her... "Did she say why?"

"Just that she couldn't go through with it." She sipped from the bottle, taking his measure while she tilted it back. "Here's the thing. Then she asked about you."

His heart picked up speed. "Did she? What did you tell her?"

"Only that you were fine. Although *fine* is a stretch." Brows raised, she studied his face. "You're not yourself. And neither is she. I could tell from the tone of her voice."

"Huh." He resisted the urge to press for details like exactly how she'd sounded when she'd asked, or if she'd asked anything else, or if she'd—He shook his head. Screw it. Who cared if he looked pathetic? Irisa had already seen him at his worst. "Did she say anything else?"

"She specifically asked if I thought you'd come to her fashion show."

"That doesn't mean she wants to see me. For all I know, she's hoping like hell that I don't show up."

"That's not true." Irisa took the bottle from his hand and set it next to hers on the counter. "Listen to me. You both have that same sad, mopey thing going on. Trust me, the way she asked was hopeful, not wary."

"You think?" The ache in his gut shifted and eased. There was only one thing to do. He pushed away from the counter. "Tell the guys I had to go. I need to pack and get on the next flight. What was the name of the hotel we stayed in? The one by Central Park?"

"You're going to New York now? You're supposed to be in Nashville in a few days for your first fan audition, remember?"

"Don't worry, I'll make it to Tennessee. But there's no way I'm waiting around until the thirteenth to see her. If there's a chance I can get her back, I'm taking it. In fact, I'll also present a proposal to her for our project. One less thing for you to worry about."

"I think I'll still worry about you. Are you sure you're going to be able to work with her that closely?"

"That's a chance I'm willing to take." He pulled up short by the door. Landry had driven him to Zander's. Shit. He pulled out his phone, ready to call a cab.

Before he could dial, Irisa dragged him by the elbow to the door, keys in hand. "Come on, I'll drive you back. With the way you're acting, I don't trust you to remember to book a hotel, let alone get on the right flight. Plus, you need help drafting the proposal."

"You rock, you know that?"

"Yeah, yeah. Flattery will get you everywhere."

He grinned. "Don't need everywhere. Just the airport."

CHAPTER TWO

Skyscrapers towered overhead, gleaming in the harsh sunlight. Luke stepped out of the cab onto the sidewalk outside Audrey Pierce Designs. He hooked his sunglasses onto his shirt collar, tried to ignore the twisting in his stomach, and swung back the glass doors to beeline for reception. Then bounded up the stairs two at a time.

A blonde woman wearing all black smiled at him. "May I help you?"

"I'm here to see Audrey."

"Your name?"

"Luke Thompson."

"Just a moment." She disappeared down a hallway.

Blondie left him plenty of time to appreciate the office digs. At least he had a lot to look at while his heart pounded through his chest. Mannequins draped in leather, sequins, chains, and denim showcased her creations. Audrey had claimed her fame dressing rock's biggest names, The Fury included. The first time he saw her, at a photo shoot for their album cover three years earlier, it was as though arrows had scored a direct shot to his heart. He'd yet to recover.

She'd been connected with Rob Hawke at the

time. The larger than life rocker had been kind to The Fury during their early years. His endorsement of Audrey's designs had made her the most sought after designer in the music industry. When Luke and Audrey had met and he'd looked into her eyes and felt her soft hand in his, he'd finally understood the phrase *love at first sight*. Or maybe *soul mate* was more accurate. All he knew was something had clicked, and the look in her eyes had suggested she'd felt it too. But he wasn't a poacher, and he liked and respected Rob too much to try to steal his woman.

Audrey's sunny personality made her instantly likable, and his band mates and Irisa had warmed up to her immediately. After that, Luke requested Audrey's clothing line for any photo shoot or tour or interview that he could. Anything to stay on her radar.

The floor creaked behind him and Luke twisted to glance down the hallway. No sign of Audrey. Hopefully, Irisa hadn't been wrong. Maybe running off like a love sick teenager hadn't been a smart idea after all. But he hadn't known what else to do. Shoving his hands into his back pockets, he wandered the room and took deep breaths of the lemon-scented air to calm his pounding heart.

Framed photos lined one wall. At the center, a picture from The Fury's photo shoot in Central Park, taken a few months earlier, caught his attention. That was the last time he'd seen her. When he'd learned she wasn't with Rob anymore, he'd convinced her to hang out with them while they played shows in New York and New Jersey. At the final show, they'd shared a private moment in the band's dressing room. He'd asked her out and she'd put on the breaks fast. *"I don't date rockers anymore."* Definitive. Final. He'd waited for her to add in that she'd still give him a chance, because it was *him*, and she'd felt their bond, but she'd remained silent. He'd been embarrassed, pissed as hell at himself that he'd either read her interest wrong or that she'd dismissed him based on his profession alone. He'd immediately shut down.

And she'd quickly moved on. To a New York suit, who was his complete and total opposite. Getting good and roaring drunk that night had been the first of many mistakes.

Soft steps sounded behind him. "Luke?"

Audrey's voice, sultry and low, spiked his heart rate into the sky. Heart in his throat, he turned.

Dark hair tumbled well past her shoulders. Light blue eyes, wide and surprised, searched his. She wore a simple black t-shirt, black shorts showcasing sexy legs, and strappy black sandals with mile high heels. The thin gold bracelets adorning her wrists jangled as she linked her fingers together.

"Hey." He managed to get out the word despite the air backing up in his lungs. Seeing her so close, something swirled deep in his core. The urge to reach out and touch her burned through his arms. He plowed his fingers through his hair and then let his hands fall to his sides.

She mirrored his stance. "What are you doing here?"

His heart fell. "I... uh... I spoke to Irisa and

thought—" Shit, this was hard. Everything he'd rehearsed on the plane sounded so stupid and trite. "I thought you'd want to talk." He sighed and raked his fingers through his hair again.

"I do. I just thought you'd call."

Okay. Better. "Not my style. As you know." He paused a moment when she didn't return his smile. He couldn't talk to her here, while her assistant hovered. "So... you want to get some coffee or something? I have a proposition to discuss with you."

Her brows arched. She opened her mouth, then glanced at her assistant, and then at the slim gold watch on her wrist. "I have a client coming in soon for a dress fitting."

That wasn't a *no*. But it also wasn't a *yes*. He inhaled a short breath that didn't help the tightness in his chest. "I can wait." His gaze flashed to one of the uncomfortable looking chairs across from Blondie's desk.

Her gaze jumped from his eyes to his lips, then back again. "Can you give me an hour? I can meet you at the coffee shop on the corner."

She'd agreed. Sweet relief eased his muscles. The sunlight streaming through the window beamed brighter. "Sure. I'll... uh... let you get back to work." Tucking his hands in his back pockets, he backed up a step toward the door. "See you soon, Sunshine."

Her eyes widened again and a tremulous smile graced her lips. "I'll see you then."

Too late, he realized what he'd said. But he didn't care so much. Before, he'd been cool and too far removed. He'd never opened up about how he'd felt and it had cost him. No more.

Now, he'd do whatever he had to do for a chance to win her heart.

***

Sunshine. Five minutes since he'd left and Audrey was still replaying that endearment over and over in her mind. He'd looked... wonderful... just as she'd remembered. Tall and muscular, dark messy hair short on the sides and longer on top, and a light beard gracing the sculpted bones of his face. The face she'd conjured in her mind countless times since they'd last met. The air between them had seemed charged—nothing new there.

She'd known by asking Irisa about Luke she might be cracking open a door, but she hadn't expected it to burst wide less than twenty-four hours later. And with some type of proposition, no less.

Nerves buzzed in her stomach, more potent than the strongest cup of coffee. She ran her fingers over the garment in front of her. The pale blue silk nearly matched Luke's eyes. Eyes she could get lost in...

Stop.

Annoyed with how easily she'd lost concentration, she snapped her attention to pulling the needle and thread through the fabric. It needed to be perfect. All of her designs did. Focusing on anything other than her business was a mistake. It was all she had. The past few years had shown her that the road to love was riddled with frustration, disappointment, and heartache.

Romance didn't work.

Romance with rockers especially didn't work.

And, that fast, Luke was back in her head. Sighing, she set aside the needle and thread and crossed the room. Her desk was cluttered with sketch books, fabric swatches, and her agenda and to-do list for her upcoming show. Behind it all, tucked into a design book, was her backstage pass from The Fury's last concert in the city. She pulled it out and ran her hand over the glossy plastic card.

The first time she'd met Luke, a connection so strong had slammed through her like she'd known him forever, even though they'd never met before. When their gazes had locked, her head had skipped a beat, but she'd been dating Rob and cheating wasn't in her make-up. Not even when their relationship hit rough times did she consider giving into impulse. Not even when it had ended and she was free to follow her heart. She'd hung out a lot with Luke on that leg of the last tour and their connection was palpable—stronger than ever. But he kept getting pulled away by the fans, the band, and the media. Just like Rob always did.

And now, Luke was here. To see her. Questions and tender thoughts swirling in her brain like thread on a spinning wheel, she placed the pass into the book and returned it to the shelf.

Renee sauntered in, blonde strands streaming over her shoulders. Her ever-efficient assistant carried a notepad and pen in one hand and a cup of tea in the other. "The caterer called to finalize the head count for the show, and the rental company needs you to sign off on one more thing."

Right. The show. The thing that she'd been throwing all her time and energy into for months. Two weeks to go, and the nerves were already building. Her first show since the breakup. Her professional collaboration with Rob Hawke had put her designs on the map and made them synonymous with rockers. Hopefully, that success would continue even though her personal relationship with him had ended.

"Thanks. I'll take care of both right away."

Renee came to a stop in front of her desk. She reached for the event checklist. "I love that you're making the show look like a rock concert."

"Putting the clothes in their element is the best way to showcase them." Everything had to go perfectly with the show. A who's who list of the top names in the music industry would be in attendance. Knocking them out of their socks was the goal. Nothing else would do.

"I'll try to keep from fan-girling all over the place. I still can't believe the bands that are coming."

Audrey stifled a groan. The last thing she needed was her assistant bouncing up to people and hounding them for an autograph. "I know you're excited. The first time can be overwhelming, especially if you're a huge fan of a certain band, but we need to be professional. This isn't just about the rock stars. If we impress the director of the domestic violence program, we'll be able to partner up with them to provide clothes for women and men starting their lives over. That means so much to me. I really want to work with them."

"Don't worry, boss. I won't embarrass you or myself. I promise." Renee held up her hand, thumb crossed over her palm. "Scout's honor."

"Thank you." She wasn't too worried. Renee might be young, but she was damn good at her job. Audrey turned back to the blue silk and picked up the needle. A peek at her watch revealed a fifteen minute wait until her client was due. Keeping busy would make the time pass faster. As she pulled the thread through the fabric, she took a deep breath, then slowly exhaled.

"So." Renee raised her brows and shifted her cup from hand to hand. "I realize I've only been working with you for a few months, but are you going to clue me in on Mister Tall, Dark, and Brooding?"

Audrey smiled at the apt description and leaned against her desk. "Luke and I have been... friends, I guess, for a while. The last time I saw him ended awkwardly."

"Sounds juicy. What happened?"

"He asked me out but I turned him down. I refuse to date another rock star."

"From what I could tell, sparks were flying between you two."

"Sparks aren't enough. It's... complicated. I hadn't heard from him since then. I have no idea what he wants to talk to me about."

"Proposition sounds intriguing. He looked pretty determined when he walked in. I guess you'll find out when you see him." Renee gathered scraps of extra material into a pile. "I can handle the fitting if you want to head over to him now."

"That's all right. I'm not flitting off anywhere. Business comes first." Audrey glanced at her watch and tapped her foot against the frustration flowing through her muscles.

Speculating about Luke was going to dominate her thoughts no matter what.

This time, she wasn't getting her hopes up.

CHAPTER THREE

The coffee shop buzzed with music and murmured conversations from the other patrons. Luke leaned back in his chair and tapped his fingers on the table. A cup of coffee sat untouched in front of him. His seat gave him full view of the window and the busy street outside. He couldn't help glancing up at every passerby.

To help distract himself, he checked his messages, sent texts to Irisa and the guys, reconfirmed his flight information for Nashville, then did his afternoon social media sweep, dropping several responses to fans' comments. He loved seeing their excitement over his interactions.

Then a tag of his name popped up.

Owen Riess Fan Page: Just heard Excite Records will be releasing a greatest hits album for The Fury. Greatest hits??? Anyway, a little bird told me the label feels the band is waning and dropped their asses. Told you, Luke Thompson. Your band is a bunch of overrated S.O.B.s. So long, suckers!

Goddamn Owen. Luke's hand clenched around his phone. He and the lead singer of Swindle Ox had never gotten along. Mutual hate was a better term. Owen had caused a lot of headaches for him and his band over the years. Someday, he'd get his. The guy was asking for it.

Within seconds, Luke's own page blew up with questions from fans begging for more information. After drumming his hands on the table for a few minutes, he crafted his reply.

Guys, The Fury has a HUGE announcement coming up soon. Something special is in the works. Stay tuned.

After making sure the band was aware of Owen's announcement, he went back to people-watching. And waiting for Audrey.

Minutes ticked by. Thirty... forty-five... a full sixty. Then fifteen more.

Unease edged through him.

She'd show up... right?

Wishing for something stronger than the coffee growing cold in front of him, he fisted the cup and swallowed some undiluted caffeine to ease his parched throat.

Finally, the door swung open and Audrey walked into the shop. She pushed her sunglasses into her hair like a headband and met his gaze. A smile flickered across her face. She waved and then turned to place her order with the barista.

His phone buzzed and he tore his eyes away from Audrey for a second. Irisa—wishing him good luck. He'd need it. He tucked his phone into his pocket as Audrey glided toward him.

"I'm sorry I'm late. My client was late and she likes to talk. A lot." She settled into the other side of the table and her perfume teased his senses. Floral with a hint of spice. He wondered if she'd taste the same.

"I'm just happy you showed up."

Tiny lines formed on her forehead. "I wouldn't stand you up."

"Good to know, Sunshine."

Slim hands clutched her iced coffee. Inches from his. "So..."

"Irisa said you broke up with that suit."

Her brows rose and he winced. *Smooth, Thompson.* Damn it. Not the way he'd intended to start.

"Dante? Yeah. I couldn't go through with it." Her thumb rubbed the base of her ring finger. He could easily picture the square-cut diamond that had once resided there.

"Why did you end things?"

She released her hold on the coffee and leaned forward, gaze direct and voice lowered. "Why are you here?"

Business first, and maybe he'd get himself together enough to talk about the rest. "The band is forming our own label."

"Did something happen with Excite?"

"Let's just say we don't see eye to eye anymore. Anyway, we're forming our own label, and we're running a contest where we're auditioning fans for a chance to win a spot in a new band that will be under our label."

"That's pretty exciting." She offered him an encouraging smile.

"We're unveiling the label news on Jett Hale's TV show in two weeks, so we'll need clothes for that, and a logo. Then, in six weeks, we're having a party in Vegas where we're announcing the winners and the new band's name. So we'll need clothes for that, too. And finally, the new band will perform on Jett's show two weeks after that, and we'll need a set design, the new band's logo designed, and clothes for the four of them and for us."

"And you want me for the clothes?"

"We want you for everything."

"Everything?" She blinked, eyes widening.

"Clothes, set design, and logos."

She sat back in her seat and blew out a breath. "I have to say the project is intriguing. I've never done set design before. Or logos, except my own."

"We know you're talented but most importantly, we can trust you. I'll be honest here, you're our first choice."

"Whoa. That's a pretty big compliment."

"So, what do you say?" He pulled out the proposal and a separate page with their payment offer. He'd researched well enough to know what would be considered fair, and then increased it by twenty percent. "You can take time to think it over. The payment amount is negotiable, too."

She read over the details and her brows arched when she looked at the amount they'd offered to pay. Then she leaned forward. "I'm in. I'm definitely up for the challenge."

"I'm glad." He extended his hand for a formal shake. When her palm pressed against his and her fingers curled around his hand, he wanted to stand up and cheer. Instead, he released her. "The guys all submitted ideas. We thought you could work off of those."

"Send me everything and I'll get started. I can have the logo for you in time for Jett's show. The timing for everything else you need should be fine once I'm finished with my own show."

"You'll be working with me. I'm handing most of this."

"That's not a problem."

"Good. Then that moves me on to the other reason I'm here." He took a deep breath and laid his hands, palm up, on the table. "I screwed up before. Big time. I was an idiot not to tell you how I felt, and I didn't want to lose another chance. As simplistic as it sounds, I like you—a lot." He reached across the table and grabbed her free hand in his. "Too damn much for me not to say anything about it. Too damn much for me to want to be with anyone else."

"Oh." Her fingers stiffened in his, but he couldn't let go.

He was already this far in—might as well finish the rest. "I'm not pulling any punches. I want to be with you. I want a relationship. With you."

Her eyes widened like saucers. A light came into them and he hoped he wasn't imagining what it meant. "You're serious."

"But what I want doesn't do any good unless you're feeling it too. I thought you were before. But maybe I was wrong." For the second time, he wished for something stronger than coffee. Alcoholic truth serum would make this easier.

Her head shook a quick no. "You weren't wrong."

He tightened his fingers around hers and

stroked his thumb in small circles over the top of her hand "No?"

"No."

She pressed her lips together for a moment. Vulnerability flashed across her face a second before it settled into the blue depths of her eyes. "You've been on my mind since the day we met."

Hearing the exact words he wanted to hear damn near made him high. A lump swelled in his throat and he had to swallow hard to speak. "You too."

"Luke..." The corners of her sweet smile drifted down and she carefully extracted her hand from his grip. The warmth in her gaze cooled. "I was serious when I said I didn't want to date a rocker again."

Even as he witnessed her barriers slide up, he couldn't believe what he was hearing. "You're crossing me off because of my career?"

"Rob was always touring, always recording. You are, too. He always put his fans first. So do you. He—"

"I'm not him."

"No. But you're always pulling out your phone to chat with the fans, or being pulled away because of the band. You've been doing that every time we've met. When we hung out during your last tour, you did it all the time."

"We owe everything to our fans. I can't ignore them."

"I'm not saying that you should ignore them, but... Damn it. That last night, you and I were having a moment in the dressing room by ourselves. Moving closer and closer together, and I really thought we'd end up kissing, but instead when Irisa knocked on the door and yelled for you to greet the fans, you pulled away then, too. If you pull away at *that* moment, what am I supposed to expect to happen in the future?"

"I'm sorry. I was an idiot. The first of many occasions where I messed up." He paused as an idea formed. "That's why you began seeing Dante, wasn't it?"

Her shoulders lifted and then fell. "He has a regular job, a regular life, and he made me feel like I was an important part of it. Everything I thought I needed, but..." Her eyes met his, needy and hungry and denying them both. "I couldn't stop thinking about you."

"I like that. I like being on your mind. I was pretty messed up for a while, thinking I'd lost you." Taking a chance, he laid his hand over hers again. Her fingers immediately curled around his.

"The three years I spent with Rob were the loneliest times of my life. I can't pretend that I don't want you, but I also can't pretend that I don't have concerns." Her bracelets clinked as she pushed her other hand through her hair. "I lived with being an afterthought with Rob for too long. I need a partnership. I want to be a priority. And I'm going to be completely honest here: I don't know if you can give me that."

He could understand her fears. Every touring musician knew how hard maintaining a relationship could be. "Will you at least give me a chance? Work with me on this project. I'm not going anywhere, unless you boot me out."

"You say that now, but what happens when this project is over?"

"You'll have to trust me. I want to be there for you. You're always on my mind, Sunshine. I'll prove to you that I'm serious."

She was quiet for a long moment. Her gaze fixed on their joined hands. He rubbed his thumb over her knuckles. Even that small motion was enough for him to feel her all the way to his toes.

Slowly, her gaze roamed from their hands, to his arms, to his chest, and then finally to his face. "Okay. But we need to go slow. Baby steps."

"I can do baby steps." He drew her hand to his face and sighed against her knuckles then planted a gentle kiss on them. "Are you free the rest of the day?"

"I have to finish up a few things at the studio. And then I want to get started on some ideas for your logo."

"How about tonight?" He'd have to plan something special. It had to be the best first date in history.

Her smile bloomed until it beamed across her face and brightened the room. "I'd like that."

They sat, sipping coffee, and talking about her upcoming show and his upcoming auditions and possible ideas for the TV show and label designs. The clouds that had been hanging over his head for months dissipated like a sky clearing after a storm. The heavy weight lifted and the sunlight of Audrey poured in.

When they drained their drinks, she glanced at her watch. "I need to get back."

"I'll walk you." He drew her to her feet. He wanted to hug her, hold her. And damn, he wanted to kiss her. But not yet. He'd have to hold back. She wanted slow. She needed to see that he wouldn't hurt her. No matter what he wanted, her needs came first.

Five hours later, he stood outside the brownstone housing her second-floor apartment. The cab idled by the curb, revving its engine every few moments, matching the beating of his heart. When Audrey came through the door, Luke nearly swallowed his tongue. He smoothed a hand down his chest and quelled the jumping sensation residing there. "You look beautiful."

The simple white dress, thin straps at her shoulders, and the way the fabric draped across her chest, hinted at curves he'd imagined far too many times. A delicate gold chain, one of her designs, with a teardrop stone the color of the ocean laid against the hollow of her throat. "Thanks. You clean up well, too. I approve of the shirt."

She should. It was from her most recent collection. "The designer's pretty special."

A blush tinted her cheeks and her lips curved in a soft smile. The need to touch her was too great to ignore. He reached out and linked their fingers and then raised her hand to his lips. More softness. More of what he'd been missing. "Ready to go?"

"Sure," her voice breathless, she glanced at the cab. "Where are we going?"

"I made a reservation at that French restaurant you told me about the last time I was in town."

"*La Chance?* I've been dying to try that place.

They're supposed to have the best desserts in the city."

He held the cab door for her and then slid in beside her. After he rattled off the restaurant address, he leaned against the seat. "I forwarded the email you sent of the preliminary logo designs to the other guys. They looked good to me. I think the black box with white font is my favorite. How was the rest of your day?"

"Busy. We only have two weeks until the show. It can get crazy up until then. I'll be putting in a lot of hours leading up to it."

"You can't be all work and no play. Maybe I can convince you to play hooky."

Her lips twitched. "I have a feeling you can be pretty persuasive."

"You have no idea." His fingers played with the ends of her hair. That rich brown cascaded around her shoulders like waves of chocolate.

She relaxed into him, letting her thigh brush against his leg and her arm rest along his side, and chatted more about the fashion show. Her face was animated, eyes sparkling when she spoke about the possibility of partnering with the domestic violence center, and the way she kept her attention on his face, as though he were far more interesting than anything passing by their window, enraptured him.

Damn, he was lucky.

The cab screeched to a stop, jolting them forward. Luke flung out his arm to protect Audrey and his elbow connected hard with her chest. Her cry echoed in his ears as his shoulder slammed into the front seat. Muttering curses, he reeled around.

"I'm sorry. Are you okay?"

"Fine." She held her hand on the red spot blooming on her sternum. Hopefully, it wouldn't bruise.

Great way to start off the evening... He paid the driver and then opened his door. "I'm happy to help make it feel better."

Her smile eased his guilt. "Maybe later you can show me what you have in mind."

Taking her hand, he led her into the crowded restaurant, anticipating candlelight, quietly efficient waiters, good wine, five-star food, and the pleasure of watching Audrey enjoy every moment.

He smiled at the hostess. "Reservation for Thompson."

She scanned her list and frowned. "I'm sorry, sir. I don't see anything here under that name."

"Can you look again? I made the reservation earlier today. When I called, the guy I spoke with said you'd had a cancellation for seven-thirty, so he put me in that slot."

"I'm sorry. There isn't anything here under that name. We're booked solid."

"How long is the wait for a table?"

"Two hours."

No way. Irritation pricked along his skin. Luke leaned in and lowered his voice, "Is there anything you can do?"

"We don't have any open tables."

"None?"

Audrey's soft cool hand curled around one of his. Her perfume teased the air and cut through his frustration. "Don't worry about it. We'll go someplace else."

"But you really wanted to try this place." All he'd wanted was a perfect night, and so far, he'd almost given her whiplash, and lost out on the romantic dinner he'd planned.

She tugged him away from the hostess. "We'll try it some other time. Come on. There's a club not too far from here. They have a lounge with pretty good food and drinks and decent live music. We can grab some food and dance."

In spite of everything, he smiled. The idea of dancing with Audrey, holding her in his arms, was way better than anything he'd dreamed. "Lead the way."

CHAPTER FOUR

The club pulsed with a hard rock beat. A throng of bodies writhed on the scarred dance floor. Audrey glanced at her dress and wrinkled her nose. Under the strobe lights, her white dress practically glowed.

In her rush to smooth out the issue at the restaurant, the club had seemed like a good idea. But now that they were here... she wondered if she'd made a huge mistake.

Luke, in his dark shirt and black pants, showcasing wide shoulders and muscles that proved he spent a solid chunk of time at the gym, blended in perfectly with the other patrons in dark colors or band t-shirts. But they'd already received a few sideways glances and her white dress was a beacon for more. Luke was bound to be recognized by at least someone, or several someones. Discomfort itched in between her shoulder blades. She wasn't big enough to block him from people's line of vision.

They sat at a little high-top table, a shared plate of nachos between them, legs tangling together. Less than eight hours ago, he'd stood in her studio, out of the blue, and now, here they were, on a date. Surreal.

He held out his beer. "Cheers."

She clinked her mojito against the brown bottle and then gestured at the club. "What do you think?"

"The acoustics are great." He leaned back in his seat and looked at the stage where three men rocked out cover versions of metal hits. "Band's not bad either."

"I love this place. Renee and I usually cap off the week with a stop here."

His fingers laced with hers on the tabletop. "I wouldn't mind coming back again."

"They occasionally get big names to play. I'm sure your band would be welcomed."

"Yeah. But I was talking about coming with you." His thumb traced a lazy circle on her palm. "Dancing with you. Holding you—"

"Excuse me." A tall man with a red and black mohawk stopped at their table. "You're Luke Thompson. Holy shit. It's really you."

"I am." Luke broke contact with Audrey's hand and held his own out toward the fan. "Good to meet you. What's your name, man?"

"Ed. Hold on. The guys aren't going to believe this." Ed waved at a group huddled by the bar and then bellowed over the music, "Luke Thompson is here!"

All eyes in the bar area and a few on the dance floor turned in their direction. Audrey shifted closer to Luke. A sense of dread filtered through along with memories of the countless times this had happened when she was with Rob. She cursed herself for being so stupid in suggesting this place. Sure enough, a mass exodus from the bar and dance floor followed. People crowded around their table like ants at a feast.

"Luke!"

"It's really him!"

"O-M-G. I'm The Fury's biggest fan."

Luke's brows rose and his smile froze on his face. His gaze connected with hers and she could see the conflict burning there. He again laced their hands together across the table. "Hey guys, it's good to meet you. Let me introduce you to my date, Audrey."

The fans gave her a cursory glance, maybe a polite nod, before they turned back to Luke with hero worship in their eyes.

Luke shook their hands, asking people's names, repeating them back. He was genuine, thanking them for their support, and joking around with them like old friends. "Thanks guys. Let me get back to my date here."

The group left, only to be replaced by new fans crowding in. Luke's posture was rigid, his hold on her hand tightening as he smiled at the fans, said hello, shook hands, then again requested they let him get back to his date with her.

Bonding over music mended gaps and broke down barriers, but the people here acted like they considered him to be family. She could understand that—music spoke to people on so many levels, and the way Luke crooned and growled lyrics made it seem like he knew exactly how the listener was feeling. No wonder they loved him.

New people flowed into the club, calling out that they'd heard about his visit through various social media sites.

Fabulous. What had she done? Stupid, stupid, stupid.

People asked him for autographs and to pose for pictures. One woman about Audrey's age thrust her phone into Audrey's hands. "You don't mind taking my picture, right? Thanks."

Audrey failed to keep her smile on her face when the woman wrapped her arm around Luke's neck and pulled him down for a kiss. He turned his head so her lips glanced off his cheek and not his mouth.

When she returned the camera to the woman, Luke slid his arm around her. "Thanks. I'm so sorry. I'm trying to get rid of them as fast as I can."

She let her hand rest on his hard stomach. He pulled her in tighter. But more people kept swarming. Fans trying to get close to Luke edged too close into her personal space. An awful, claustrophobic feeling clawed at her skin.

Luke must have noticed. "Guys, can we back up? My date and I need some breathing room."

A small space opened, but soon was crowded with people again. This was ridiculous. She leaned toward his ear. "I'm going to the bar."

His lips tightened. "Give me five minutes to clear this out, then we'll leave."

"Okay."

Luke's hold loosened and then fell away as he shook more hands and posed for more pictures. The tightness in Audrey's chest eased as she retreated further and further away from the crowd and took a seat at the bar. The high stool gave her a good vantage point and the fresh mojito gave her time to sip and decide that saying yes to Luke had been a mistake.

Luke did glance around a few times, perhaps looking for her, but people kept approaching him from every angle. He made an effort to speak to everyone. Even the band on stage joined in when they finished their set.

Audrey glanced at her watch. Half an hour of sitting back was enough. The spot on her chest throbbed. Whether from its earlier contact with Luke's elbow, or disappointment, she couldn't tell. But she'd reached a decision.

After one last sip of her drink, she pushed her way through the crowd, but three-deep out, people wouldn't budge and she couldn't move any further. She peered over tall shoulders. Thankfully, her heels made her tall enough for Luke to spot her.

He motioned for her and spoke words that were swallowed up by the crowd. They shifted and let her through.

"Hey." Smiling, he wrapped his arm around her. The heat of his skin felt good, tempting her to relax into him, but she held herself stiff. "I'm sorry about this. Someone on my fan page announced I was doing a flash meet-and-greet here."

"I'm going to take off."

"Wait." Hands on her shoulders, he drew her closer and leaned down, searching her face. "Please."

She shook her head. "I've already waited. You're having a good time here, and obviously, this is important to you."

"You're important, too."

Was she? She wondered... "I think it's wonderful that you take the time to talk to each person and make them feel valued. But you're so busy with that, there isn't any time for one-on-one for you and me. So, you stay. I'll go. I've already called a cab. It should be outside now." She'd received the confirmation for cab pick-up while sitting at the bar.

He grabbed hold of her hand, preventing her retreat. "I'm sorry it got out of control."

"It's fine. Really. I have to get up early tomorrow anyway." Watching his eyes, memorizing how they looked up close, she fought against the stab of loss in her gut. "I'll wait to hear back from you and the guys about the design sketches. Maybe we can meet up the next time you're in town. Or you can meet with my assistant. Have Irisa call me with the band's availability for meeting up to pick out clothes before the TV show."

A frown marred his brow. "It's only Tuesday. I'm not leaving for Nashville until Friday night."

"I have a lot going on with my show." She didn't want to have this conversation here, in murmured tones in full view of over a hundred people. "And, honestly, I need a few days to think about things."

"Audrey." His grip tightened and he pulled her closer. "I'll give you those few days, but I'll be back on Sunday. I'm sticking around, Sunshine."

She lifted her head until her lips were by his ear. "This is exactly what happened when we hung out during your last tour. You're never going to be able to put a relationship first. I went through what happened tonight with Rob too many times, too."

He glowered at Rob's name and then faced the crowd, raising his voice so it carried through the room, "Guys, I'm so glad I got to meet you. Now, if you'll excuse me, I really need to get back to my date."

The groans and complaints and disappointment on several of the fans' faces tugged at her. "Don't," she whispered against his cheek. "Now I feel like a shrew. And they'll all blame me if you leave."

"I want to be with you."

"I want to be with you too. But sometimes, we don't get what we want, or what we want isn't what's best for us." She brushed a kiss over his beard and pulled her hand out of his grip. "Be happy."

Then, she turned to the crowd. "Don't worry. You guys get to have him. I'm not pulling him away."

"Audrey..."

With a cheery wave, she darted into the throng. When she reached the door, she turned back. The crowd had swallowed up her space, pressing around Luke, all talking at once. He stared at her, face like stone.

Biting her lip, she stepped out into the night. She couldn't let him sway her. If she did, she'd only end up hurting them both.

***

Late Saturday morning, Luke strolled through

downtown Nashville with Ivan, one of the band's roadies who was also filling in as his cameraman to record the audition. They rounded a street corner and passed a man strumming a guitar and singing a song about love gone wrong.

Luke could relate.

No contact with Audrey for four days, except the lone email with the approved logo design, ticked him off. His screw up at the club ticked him off even more. Irisa's early words of advice echoed in his head, *"You can't please all of the people all of the time."*

No shit.

But he'd failed at pleasing the one person who mattered most. Her experience with Rob had caused scars, and her experience with Luke at the club had apparently reopened those wounds. He had to fix what had happened there. How could he make her understand how nervous he was about fucking up everything with the fans? How every interaction could make or break him and how guilty he felt about everything that had happened before. He was stuck between a rock and a hard place in trying to please everyone. No excuse though, he'd have to try harder.

Sweat trickled down his back. He stepped inside the cool comfort of an air-conditioned coffee shop. A large iced coffee helped chase the cobwebs of fitful sleep. He bought Ivan the same and then checked his messages. Nothing from Audrey. Jayne had sent him information on the first contestant, Hugh Tremont, a recent college grad who had been singing and playing guitar for fifteen years.

Cool. Life-long musicians were his type of people.

"Luke." A shaggy-haired blond guy wearing an old Fury concert t-shirt approached his table. "I'm Hugh."

"Hey, man." He shook hands. "Want anything to drink?"

"How cool is this, Luke Thompson is buying me coffee." He smiled at Ivan and introduced himself. They exchanged hellos and Luke made sure they were both fueled with coffee.

"We're going to one of the conference rooms at the hotel. We'll hang out and talk and then listen to you sing. Okay?"

Hugh nearly bounced on his toes. "Sure. Yes. Fine. Thanks."

Luke laughed and clapped him on the back. "Relax, man. It's too early for that much energy." He led the way into the harsh sunlight and back to the hotel. When they arrived in the conference room, he nodded to Ivan to start rolling.

Luke stood next to Hugh at the table and waved to the camera. "Hi, Fury fans. Luke here, with our first singer contestant for the New Band Contest. Everyone, meet Hugh. Hugh, say hello."

Hugh blushed deep red. "Hey, guys."

"How long have you been playing music?"

"Since I was a kid. Age five for singing, and ten years old for guitar."

"Cool. And the song you submitted in your demo was *Lights Out*. We're ready to hear you rock it." He took a seat. "Show me what you've got."

They waited a full minute. Hugh's hands were

shaking and his cheeks flushed scarlet. He opened his mouth but no words came out. Then, he shook himself. "Sorry, guys."

He rubbed his hands over his face. Took another quick breath, and opened his mouth, but again no words came out.

Luke nodded. "Relax, bud. It's cool. Try again."

And... Hugh looked at him, took a breath, opened his mouth, and... nothing.

Luke exchanged a glance with Ivan and frowned. How serious was this case of stage fright? "You okay, Hugh?"

"Sorry, I guess it's nerves." Hugh shoved his hair out of his face. "I don't usually get like this. But you're *you*. I didn't even get this nervous when I met Rob Hawke at his show last month."

At Rob's name, Audrey flashed into Luke's mind. Just the mention of Rob nearly set him off. If it weren't for Rob, Audrey wouldn't be jaded against him. He had to fix what had happened. Right now. Luke bolted up out of his chair and two sets of eyes pinned him in place. Much as he wanted, no needed, to make things right with Audrey, he couldn't run out on Hugh. Not when the kid reminded him so much of himself.

"I'm... sorry." The young singer stood at the center of the room, shoulders hunched, staring at the floor.

Luke murmured to Ivan, "Cut the recording."

Setting aside his coffee, Luke rose. Zander had recently begun mentoring a young guitarist. Luke was more than happy to do something similar here. "Hugh, you're fine, bud. Take a deep breath, hold it for four counts and then let it out in eight counts. And then do it again. Do you know the words to *Cut Down*?"

One of The Fury's most well-known songs, thanks to use in commercials and a popular video game, it had a good beat and would suit Hugh's voice well.

In the midst of the slow exhale, Hugh nodded.

"Cool. We're singing it together." He queued it up in his phone, joined Hugh, and patted his shoulder. "If you get nervous, just close your eyes. That always helped me. Then, it isn't any different than singing in the shower."

"Do *you* still get nervous?" Interest overtook embarrassment and Hugh looked Luke straight in the eyes.

"Hell, yeah. I have to do breathing exercises before every show to calm down. Hook me up with your email address and I'll send them to you. I'll also show them to you when we're finished for the day."

"Thanks, man. I really want this opportunity. I don't usually get nervous, but it's *you*. You're my idol." Hugh's grateful smile touched off one of his own. Being able to fix something made him feel better.

When their cue came, he started and Hugh joined in, eyes closed for several beats. The kid had a decent voice. Halfway through, he relaxed enough to look at Luke. Luke smiled and nodded and gave him a thumbs up. Nerves still lurked, but not enough to freeze him. By the time the last note faded, Hugh was grinning.

So was Luke. "That was awesome, man. Now can you sing *Lights Out*?"

Hugh nodded.

Luke returned to his seat and gestured for Ivan to begin recording again. And Hugh belted out the lyrics in perfect pitch.

Luke wasn't sure who was more proud when the song finished—Hugh or him. "Fuck yeah, man. Now that's the way to do it."

Hugh accepted Luke's high-five with a huge grin. "Thanks, Luke. I appreciate the support. Can I take you guys to lunch or something?"

"Lunch is good. My treat, though." He liked Hugh and wanted some extra time to see if the kid would mesh well with his band mates.

Throughout lunch, his phone buzzed with message alert after message alert but none were from Audrey. Too many times during the past few days, he'd drafted messages to her only to later delete them. Once he got home, they were going to talk. And like it or not, he wasn't leaving until she listened.

CHAPTER FIVE

Audrey trudged into her apartment, thoughts as dark as the clouds rolling across the nighttime sky. The scent of impending rain hung heavy in the air. She was in the mood for a good, drenching thunderstorm. A full Saturday spent at the studio, without Renee, had been exhausting. Her assistant was down for the count with a nasty head cold, and she'd been left dealing with last-minute issues for the show, chasing down two misplaced invoices, and working a fourteen-hour day with battered concentration thanks to a construction crew working on the shop next door.

She cranked up the A/C, shed her work clothes, pulled on a yellow tank top and denim cut-offs, and wound her hair into a messy topknot. Slowly, the tension seeped out of her system.

Sketchbook in hand, she padded barefoot into the living room and settled onto the chair by the window for her Saturday night ritual of sketching new designs. As raindrops pelted the window, her pencil formed quick lines across the page. Not clothes or more logo designs for Furious Records— a sketch of Luke's face.

He was due back from Nashville on Sunday afternoon. She'd thought about him constantly since that night at the club. Missing him didn't mean she should contact him, or that being involved was the best thing for them. Best to leave their relationship professional.

Brendan, Landry, Zander, and Luke had all signed off on one of the logo designs. Luke had forwarded the email to her two days earlier. She still wanted to give them a few more options. Turning to a blank page, she sketched the name in all caps, then added aggressive strokes underneath. Then played with different borders—squares, circles, shaded boxes. Eventually, she'd move to the design software in her computer. But for her, starting by hand was always best.

The door buzzer sounded, jarring her out of her musing. Who would be out there at ten o'clock at night? She set her sketch pad aside and pressed the *talk* button. "Yes?"

"It's me." Luke's voice rumbled through the speaker.

Her pulse jumped. Her hands flew to her hair and met the hasty knot. Damn it, she wasn't ready. "Come on up."

She spent the next minute rushing around her apartment, trying to decide whether to straighten up her place or her appearance. Too soon, a knock sounded. Heart beating fast, she opened the door.

Raindrops dotted Luke's blue t-shirt. His quietly assessing gaze traveled down her body and up in one smooth move. "You're always in heels. I didn't realize how small you are without them."

She resisted the urge to defend her height or apologize for her super casual appearance. Though, from the way he was looking at her, he didn't seem to mind. "I thought you weren't coming back until tomorrow."

"I was able to get on an earlier flight." He shifted his hold on his travel bag.

"Oh." She bit her lip then stepped back and gestured to her living room. "Want to come in?"

"I didn't take a cab all the way over here from the airport just to stand in the hall."

"If you're going to be sarcastic, you can get back in that cab and leave."

He inched closer without crossing the threshold and loosely entwined his fingers between hers. "I'm sorry. It's been a long day. A long several days. And a miserable flight. I do want to come in."

She nodded and stepped back, maintaining their tenuous connection. Keeping hold of her hand, he followed her over the threshold and shut the door at his back.

"Can I have my hand back now?"

"I like it where it is." He dropped his bag on the floor and raised their joined hands to his lips and kissed her fingers.

The sensation traveled all the way to her toes. She couldn't give in to it. "Luke."

He opened her hand and his lips kissed her palm and then moved to her wrist. The roughness of his beard added to the tingling. "Your pulse is jumping."

"Maybe I'm angry."

His blue eyes stared into hers. He lifted an eyebrow and then gave her a half-smile. "Maybe you are. Maybe it's something more. Maybe you want to see what it's like if I kiss you."

Her lips parted and her gaze fell to his mouth.

"Because I want to see what it's like." His other hand caressed the bare skin of her forearm.

She wanted to back up, but somehow her back was against the door, and he was so wonderfully near. "No."

"Why not?"

"Because I might..." They needed to talk. This physical reaction didn't solve anything.

He shifted until mere inches separated them. "You might what?"

Hell, she'd have to be honest. "I might not want to stop."

***

Luke stared into the wide blue eyes gazing up at him. Audrey's chest rose and fell in fast breaths. He inhaled, and her subtle spicy floral scent beckoned him closer. "I might not want to stop either. In fact, I know I won't. What's wrong with that?"

"It's not the answer."

"Maybe it's the only answer."

Her gaze jumped from his eyes to his mouth, then back and forth again. She lifted her hand to his chest and her fingers tightened, gripping his shirt. Vulnerability swirled in her eyes and she bit her lip. He knew that look—hesitation and consideration. He lowered their joined hands to his side and raised his other hand to cup her cheek.

Audrey's lips parted and her head tilted into his

palm.

He leaned down, until they were a breath apart, and then hovered, savoring the anticipation. He'd been waiting three years for this moment. They'd only get one first kiss.

Her hand tugged on his shirt, pulling him in. Luke closed the distance. Audrey's lips were as soft as silk and as warm as spiced cider. He tasted a trace of vanilla. Like his favorite double-shot espresso coffee, she spiked his blood. When her tongue met his, he groaned and slanted his lips, seeking more access. Wet strokes drove his need higher, and then Audrey dragged his lower lip between her teeth. He leaned more of his weight into her, desperate to get closer.

Her body, warm and lush, molded to his form. With a soft sigh, she released his shirt to touch his neck, and then dug her fingers into his hair. Her other hand traced patterns on his back as she explored his muscles.

The light touches and firmer holds drove him crazy. He needed more. Now.

His hand glided from her cheek, down her side, bypassing the curves he intended to slowly uncover when need wasn't wrecking his concentration. He found the small of her back and the strip of skin where her waistband met the bottom hem of her shirt. A teasing bit of skin. Soft. Warm. Sexy.

Audrey went lax when his fingers stroked that spot. She broke the kiss and leaned her head against the door. "So good."

He lifted his gaze from the pulse jumping in her neck and smiled at the blissed-out ease in her expression. He flexed his hand, fingers spread wide, over her skin, covering more of that satin-softness. She arched her back, pressing her torso into his, and he didn't try to hide how much she'd affected him—from the full length of his arousal, to his shaking hands, and his racing heartbeat.

On a moan, her eyes opened. She watched him as her hips lifted and pressed into his. He held her there while his pulse throbbed and his blood hummed.

She'd completely rocked his world with that kiss. Could she really walk away from their connection? Before things went too far, he needed to make sure they were on the same page. He eased back, until they were no longer touching anywhere except the hands joined at his side. "We need to talk."

"We do." She looked as dazed as he felt. "Want some wine?"

He nodded and followed her through her tiny apartment. Audrey's space was exactly like her—understated and elegant. An oversize open bookcase filled with tons of design books and colored glass bowls split the room in half, dividing living room and bedroom. Gauzy pale pink curtains surrounding the bed allowed even more privacy for her sleeping space.

Through the curtains, the bed, soft and white like a cloud, was covered with pale pink pillows. He pictured them on the bed, enclosed in the sheer seclusion, as he worshiped her body. But they'd never get there if they didn't hash out their problem here.

As his body reacted to his horizontal fantasy, he turned his attention back to the living room. Several dark frames in various sizes decorated the white walls. Throw pillows dotted with sequins lined the deep brown couch. His fantasy switched to them laying on the couch. Damn it, he could picture them together everywhere. He adjusted his jeans and followed her into the kitchen.

The kitchenette was one-tenth the size of the kitchen in his home. Audrey poured white wine into two stemless wine glasses. On the counter, a large bouquet of red roses spilled out of an overfilled crystal vase. The sweet fragrance filled the small space.

"Who sent you the flowers? A satisfied client?" Shit. He'd never sent flowers after she'd designed something for him. Paid promptly—always. Recommended her to others—all the time. Extra thanks through flowers—no.

A blush crept into her cheeks and then she frowned at the vase. "Not exactly. But it's not a big deal."

He didn't like that answer. Without waiting for her to offer more information, he plucked the card from the blooms and read the note. *Love can grow. - Dante*

Muscles tensed, he fought to release his tight jaw. He dropped the note on the counter and pictured finding the guy and shoving the thorny stems down his throat. "Why is he sending you flowers?"

"I don't know. They arrived yesterday. I haven't spoken to him since we broke up."

What if his actions at the club caused her to want to run back to Dante? His gut twisted at the idea of life without her again. But if that was what she wanted, he'd have to find a way to let her go. "Answer me this—do you want to get back together with him?"

She shook her head without hesitation. "No."

The tension in his chest eased. "Then why keep the flowers?"

"I like flowers and it seemed a waste to throw them away."

"You don't have a neighbor who might enjoy them?" He realized he was being a dick the second the words left his mouth.

A frustrated sound worked free from her throat. "Except for the day you arrived, I've been working fourteen-hour days for the past two weeks. Excuse me for being too exhausted for that idea to occur to me." Abandoning the wine, she stepped around him and stalked into the living room.

He followed, and then stopped at the sight of her sitting on the couch, rubbing her temples. She looked exhausted. How had he missed the dark circles under her eyes? The anger drained out of him. "I don't want to fight with you."

"Me either." With a sigh, she lowered her hands. "I'm sorry the roses upset you. I'll get rid of them in the morning."

That sounded promising... He sank onto the cushion beside her. "Does that mean you've had time to think about us?"

"With the way we left things the other night... Even up until tonight, I really didn't know what to do. I don't want to hurt either of us. I couldn't say much of anything at the club because I was in front of the fans and didn't want my words splashed all over the internet. But we're alone now. I want the man I'm with to actually be with me. What the heck am I supposed to do if you keep putting the fans first?"

"I should've done a better job about keeping you with me. I also should've been better about cutting short the time I spent with the fans. It's not an excuse, but after all that happened on the last tour, I'm afraid of doing something that might further strain the fans' relationship with the band." He shrugged and then sighed. "And, I always think about how there might be one person who really needs to see me, and how it might really matter that we talked. Fans have told us as much, and I like feeling like I've made a positive difference, especially when I've been in the headlines too many times for the wrong reasons."

Hands clasped, she studied him for a long moment. "I feel sort of the same way when someone tells me that something I've designed makes them feel the best they've ever felt about themselves. You do make a difference with your music. You touch a lot of people. I don't want to stand in your way or stop you from doing what you need to do. But I also need to feel like I'm a priority in your life. You know what happened with Rob. I won't go through that again. "

He rested his hand over hers on her lap. "In trying to fix my mistakes with the fans, I keep creating more with you. You're more important than anyone else. I promise to be better about keeping our time as our time."

"I'm going to hold you to that. A relationship means putting each other first. Yes, we both have demanding jobs and obligations, but we need to put each other first. If we don't, that's a deal breaker for me."

"I want to be the man you need. Please let me show you that I can be." He wanted to see her smile, and fuck, he needed to hold her again. "Next time, I'll handcuff myself to you so the mob can't come between us. Or if we really need some privacy, we can wear disguises."

Her lips curved in the start of a smile. "When you say that, I'm picturing you in a fedora and trench coat, like one of those hard-boiled detectives in a nineteen-thirties movie."

"I wouldn't mind seeing you in a trench coat, especially if you wore nothing underneath it." He wiggled his brows at her and she tossed one of her throw pillows at his head. Pale pink sequins attached to the fuzzy pillow struck his chin and tangled in his beard.

He counter-attacked, lobbing a pillow in her direction, and landing a hit. She came at him with a one-two punch, a pillow in each hand, scoring a hit on his head and stomach. A blur of arcing pillows followed, raining down upon him. He counted at least ten—how many did she have? He gave as good as he got, tossing the soft missiles back as soon as they landed.

Laughing, panting, Audrey spun away and snatched a large white pillow from the chair by the window. She launched onto the couch, aiming for his side.

In defense, Luke grabbed her around the waist and rolled her beneath him. He locked his hands around her wrists and pressed her arms over her head, into the pillows he'd stockpiled at the end of the couch. "Give up."

She blew a stray hair out of her face and gave a defiant toss of her head. "Never."

He grinned down at her as lightning flashed outside the window and rain battered the windows and thunder rumbled across the sky. "I missed you, Sunshine."

"I missed you, too."

"Are we good? I'm so sorry I messed up that night."

"We're good. Better, actually, now that we understand each other more." She tugged her arms from his grasp and then wound them around his back. "I'm glad you're here."

He nuzzled her neck. "Can I spend the night?"

She sighed when his lips met the soft skin by her ear and tilted her head to give him better access. "To sleep, yes. Nothing else. I still want to take things slow. I know we agreed on baby steps, and I think that's a good idea."

"We can go slow. As long as I can lie beside you and hold you, I'll be happy." He needed to feel her in his arms, to lie beside her and breathe her in. Reversing their positions, he rolled until he was cradling her body with his, then massaged her back and neck in slow circles. Easing the tension, feeling her soften, taking care of her in a tiny way, and hopefully showing her just how much the second chance meant to him.

CHAPTER SIX

Audrey slipped slowly toward sleep while Luke rubbed the tension right out of her body. Rain continued to pound against the window. Another bolt of lightning lit across the sky, quickly followed by a resounding boom of thunder rattling the windows. She tightened her hold on him and then laughed. "That was louder than I expected."

"I'm just glad I'm not out there. Warm and dry is better. Warm and dry with you is better still."

Stifling a yawn, she stretched against his muscular frame. "It's getting late."

His fingers traced her face. "You look exhausted."

"I've been working more than anything else. And sleep hasn't been easy."

He dropped a kiss on her lips, then rolled off of her and extended his hand to help her to her feet. "We'll both sleep better tonight."

"Unless you hog the blankets, pillows, or mattress."

Hand in hand, they walked to the bedroom area. She refused to let nerves set in. They weren't doing anything other than sleeping, but sleep in itself was a vulnerable thing. When he ducked into the bathroom with his bag, she pulled out a tank top and sleep shorts and changed clothes, then flipped off the lights. He came out wearing his t-shirt and boxers.

"Be right back." She slipped by him, trading places, and zipped through her nighttime routine.

When she emerged, he stood by the bed. He'd turned down the covers and clicked on her bedside lamp. "You have a side preference?"

"The left. Closest to the window."

"Good. I like being closest to the door."

She slid into soft, cool sheets and hard, hot Luke. The perfect combination.

He switched off the light and slipped his arm around her waist. They lay there in the dark, listening to the patter of rain and talking about their days.

For the first time in a long time, she fell asleep feeling complete.

Audrey woke up to sunlight streaming in the windows. The sheer pink curtains gave a rose-colored tint to the room. The heavy weight of Luke's arm was a solid band, locking her to him. She glanced at the clock and then rolled to face him.

Sleepy blue eyes blinked open. "Good morning, Sunshine."

"Hi. It won't be morning for much longer. We slept in pretty late." She traced a finger along his beard. "Sleep okay?"

He grunted an assent and tucked the pillow under his head. "You don't have to work today, do you?"

"Just a quick meeting this afternoon with one of

the models for my show. She's been away on a magazine shoot and I need her to try on her outfit one more time."

His fingers skated along her spine. She shivered against the sensation and wiggled closer to him. "Then here's the plan, we get up, shower, coffee, and then we're picking up breakfast at the cafe near the park."

"And eating it at the park?"

"Yeah." He nipped at her lip. "Then I'll watch you do your fashion designer thing, and then you're mine for the rest of the day."

"Sounds like a pretty good deal to me." She cuddled in for a moment and then forced herself to roll out of bed. "Okay, let's go. You can shower first. I'll start the coffee."

While the coffee brewed, Audrey stuck the roses into a large tote bag. She'd drop them off to her downstairs neighbor on the way to breakfast. Dante would be expecting a response to the roses. Calling him now wouldn't work. She didn't want to upset Luke.

The sound of his singing drew her into the living room. She smiled. He really did have a great voice. And the cheesy love songs he'd chosen made her laugh. If only the hard rock world could hear him now.

The pipes squeaked as the water stopped. Audrey grabbed her coffee and rifled through her closet. The day promised to be a scorcher. She needed something light and cool and as happy as her mood.

Luke joined her, wrapping his arms around her

waist. He wore a white t-shirt and faded gray shorts. She pulled out gun-metal gray metallic sandals and a white cotton sundress with bold purple flowers splashed across the skirt. "Did you save me any hot water?"

"Some. We'd save more if you joined me next time." His teeth sunk into the curve between her shoulder and neck.

She shivered as awareness tingled up her spine. "If you throw in another private concert like today's, I might consider it."

"You liked my medley for you, huh?"

Twisting to face him, she grinned. "Loved it. I'll take an encore anytime."

A short time later, they sat sprawled on the Great Lawn in Central Park enjoying their breakfast picnic of bagels, fruit, and iced coffee. He'd been recognized at the cafe, and again as they strolled by the park's boat pond. Both times, he'd kept his hand on her arm, shoulder, or waist, and introduced her to the fans.

He'd done everything to make her feel included. If she were keeping score, he'd be even date-wise, one-to-one. Time would tell on which side he'd predominately fall. She fed him a grape, then leaned back on her hands and stared at the sky. "Today's been a nice breather. It'll get me through the next six days until the show."

"Nervous?"

"Every time. But especially this time. So much is riding on it. Not only is it the first one I'm doing post-Rob, but I really want to show the domestic violence program's director that I'm the right designer for this project. The model I'm meeting with later today was in an abusive relationship a few years ago and so this is something very close to my heart. So, yeah, I'm pretty nervous about this show going well."

"I'll be there." He shifted until they were shoulder to shoulder and intertwined their fingers on the grass. He said it easily, like her depending on him was a given, like he wouldn't let her down.

She rested her head on his shoulder. "Maybe next Sunday we can do this again. The show will be over then, and I'll know the director's decision, and I'll need to decompress."

"Irisa, Jayne, and the guys will still be in town then too."

"It'll be good to meet Jayne and see everyone else again." Her watch winked in the sunlight. She glanced at the time and calculated the distance to her studio. "We'd better go. I don't want Vanessa to be stuck outside waiting for me."

"That's the model, right?"

"She's also become a good friend. She stayed with me for a while after she left that bad relationship. Anyway, her fitting won't take too long. Her new boyfriend is in town with her, so I'm sure she has things she'd rather be doing with him."

Luke gathered the remains of their picnic. "Probably the same type of things I want to do with you."

"Luke." Heat crept across her cheeks.

Grinning, he reached for her hand. "Come on, Sunshine, let's get you to the old salt mine."

"Vanessa asked me to design some things for

him too. He's a rocker. I wonder if you know him."

"What's his name?"

"He plays in a band called..." She scrunched her forehead, trying to remember. "Ox something or other."

He stopped walking. "Swindle Ox?"

"That's it. I'm not sure which guy in the band she's dating."

"Their lead singer is an ass. The other guys aren't as bad as him." He fell in step beside her again. "I really hope it's not Owen."

"Why?"

"He's the asshole who hacked into our fan club a few months ago, posing as me, announcing that I was leaving the band."

"Oh." That incident had happened a week after the band had wrapped up their tour. She remembered reading about it and the PR nightmare it had caused for Irisa. The announcement had created a giant headache for everyone in the band.

"Well, in that case, I hope it's not him either."

When they arrived at the shop, he held the door for her, and followed her inside. "If Renee isn't better by tomorrow. I'll come in and help you."

She sighed at the state of her to-do list. "Thanks. I may take you up on that offer."

They both turned as the door opened. Vanessa glided in, tall and tan and glowing. A tall man followed behind. Audrey rushed to hug her. "You look fabulous."

"That's what the Caribbean will do for you." Vanessa stepped back and raised her brows at Luke. "This is..."

"Luke Thompson." Audrey placed her hand on Luke's arm, excited for them to meet.

Beside her, he vibrated and growled like an angry dog on a tight leash. "What the hell are you doing here?"

Audrey blinked at his rudeness. His words and gaze weren't directed at Vanessa, but at the glowering man by her side.

The man rolled his brawny shoulders and closed in on Luke. "What's it to you,"—he sneered with an exaggerated curled lip—"candy-assed shit-bag?"

Tension snapped and crackled between the men staring each other down like boxers before a fight. Luke's fingers flexed at his sides and his jaw went rigid as a stone.

She glanced from them to Vanessa. Her friend shrugged. "I take it you two know each other."

"We go way back," Luke snapped out, his stare frozen on the other man.

She'd never seen him quite so *angry*. All hopes for a stress-free afternoon vanished. Her caring, brooding man had morphed into a vengeful, seething fighter.

And it looked like Luke was about to collect payback.

***

Luke's hands clenched into fists. He and the front man for Swindle Ox shared a mutual hate of each other. The feud had started years ago with a slighted Owen blaming Luke for an upset at a music awards show and showed no signs of stopping.

The fact they had girlfriends who apparently were friends? Fucking nightmare.

Audrey stepped in between them. "Vanessa, come on back with me. Guys, I get that you don't like each other but this is a place of business. If you can't be civil, then please leave."

Vanessa slipped her hand into Owen's. "Come on, baby. Be nice."

"To him? No way." He glanced at Audrey, and then sneered at Luke. "Still with your band?"

Luke moved in front of Audrey. "Why? Thinking of starting any new fake rumors? Come at my fans' space again and I'll take you down so fast your head will spin."

"What are you—the fan club police?"

Luke's muscles burned with the urge to punch the smirk right off of Owen's face. "I'm the guy who's going to rearrange your fucking face if you do one more thing to mess with me or my fans."

"Luke." Audrey's hand tugged the back of his shirt. He hadn't realized he'd moved a step in Owen's direction.

"What." He spat out the word as he turned toward her. The tunnel vision he'd had slowly expanded to include his surroundings. The clothes, the photos on the wall, the light lemon scent, but most clear of all was the confusion and unhappiness on Audrey's face.

"Let's go." Her hand linked with his and she drew him toward the door. "Go get a coffee or something. I won't have bloodshed on my floors."

"You're kicking *me* out?" He stopped walking.

After all they'd shared last night, he couldn't believe she didn't have his back. "What about him?"

"I need to check Vanessa's dress and then fit him for two shirts and a pair of pants. I can't do that with the two of you having a pissing contest."

He dipped his head low until his lips met her ear and then his whispered through gritted teeth, "I don't want to leave you with him here."

Audrey peered at Owen and Vanessa for a moment and he followed her gaze. His nemesis had his arm around the tall, tan model, playing the part of adoring boyfriend. "What he did to you wasn't right, but he doesn't seem so bad."

"Trust me, he is."

She nudged him closer toward the door. "I have experience handling moody rockers. Give me a half-hour, forty-five minutes tops. I'll call you when the coast is clear."

Behind Audrey's back, Owen flipped him off. Shaking his head, Luke strode out of the shop and headed for a hit of caffeine that wouldn't do a damn bit of good. Sucking down icy black coffee with two shots of espresso, he walked the neighborhood until the urge to throttle Owen lessened to the level of possibly being in the same room with him without punching his lights out.

When Audrey's call came forty minutes later, he'd calmed down enough to realize he shouldn't have let Owen bait him. He returned to the studio and found her standing in the front room of the shop. Her serious expression didn't harbor any hint of a smile. His gaze swept the space. What he was looking for, he didn't know, but Owen always put him on edge. "You okay?"

She set down her phone on a glossy white table. "You've been in a few fights recently."

He'd been in a few scraps lately, and admittedly, at least one was his fault, but he never went off half-cocked without a damn good reason. "So?"

"So, I didn't want another one to break out in the middle of my studio. You guys looked like you were ready to tear each other's heads off."

"Likely were." But she looked far too upset for his comfort, and that wasn't okay. Remorse trickled through him, shaming the angry beast within. He cupped his hands over her shoulders. Stiffened muscles met his palms. "And I apologize. Owen and I have a lot of bad blood between us. He gets under my skin."

"I noticed. How did this feud start?"

"We were both nominated for the same award a few years ago. The Fury won and he thought his band should have. He was pretty vocal about it. Then, one of the online rock magazines held a weekly head-to-head contest for lead singers. He and I were going against each other. Again, I won and he got pissed off. We've had some interesting exchanges since then. Some were minor pranks, and a lot of trash-talking, but that incident with the fan club and my supposed leaving the band went too far."

"Aren't you guys with the same record label?"

"We were before Excite released my band. That doesn't mean we have to like each other." He massaged the tension knotting her muscles. "But I shouldn't have done anything here. That wasn't cool. Again, I'm sorry."

"Apology accepted. Just promise me that you guys can get along at the fashion show."

His fingers tightened on the muscles he'd just finished soothing. "He's going to be there?"

"Since Vanessa is modeling, he said he'd come. He'll know a lot of the attendees."

"Hmm." The last thing he wanted was to be stuck in a room with Owen. At least he'd have his guys there to hold him back if necessary.

Her hands slid from his hips to his chest. "Luke, this show is really important to me. I don't want to have to worry about you and Owen on top of everything else."

"I promise I'll do my best to not kill him." He placed a gentle kiss on her forehead. "You don't have to worry about that."

Finally, her smile returned. "Good."

The jangling tune of Audrey's cell phone filled the air. He glanced at the screen and her shoulders stiffened again. A sigh escaped her lips. "That's Dante's number."

He bit back a growl. "I'll leave if you want privacy."

"You can stay." Remaining in the circle of his embrace, she held the phone to her ear. "Hello."

"Audrey, how are you?" A deep voice with a hint of an Italian accent came through the speaker, as loudly as if Audrey had put the phone on speaker.

"I received the roses you sent."

"They made me think of you, *bella*. I hope you

liked them."

"They're beautiful... but remember that rocker I told you about?" She raised her gaze to his face and smiled. Her small hand tightened further around his back, securing her hold. Luke leaned into her touch.

Silence reigned for a long moment, and then Dante sighed. "Luke, right?"

"Right. The thing is, we just started seeing each other."

"I see." Another long pause followed. "Well, I hope it works out the way you want it to."

Luke shook his head at the voice coming out of the receiver. The guy answered like a true suit, without backbone and giving up without a fight. Not that Luke wanted him to fight, but Dante wasn't any kind of man in his book. Audrey deserved better.

"Thank you. Me too." She cuddled in closer until the warmth of her body mingled with his. Luke rubbed his hand up and down her back. She was smart, beautiful, talented, and kind—damn, he was lucky.

Dante continued, "You're special, Audrey. Make sure he treats you that way."

"I will. I hope you find what you're looking for, too." She ended the call and set the phone on the table. "There, all settled."

He hoped so. "Think that's enough to make sure he gets the message you're not available?"

"Yes. He really is a good guy, you know."

"He can be someone else's guy. Not yours."

She pulled him down for a kiss. "I have my hands full with you anyway."

He wrapped his arms around her and deepened the kiss. Having her hands full with him was one thing. Being a distraction to her was another. He'd find a way to deal with being around Owen. No way would he disappoint Audrey again.

CHAPTER SEVEN

Luke spent most of Wednesday huddled in the back room of Audrey's studio. They finalized the few tweaks she'd made to the Furious Records logo and began discussing color and texture preferences for the launch party in Vegas. She'd been working non-stop for days, going from The Fury's business to her preparations for the show, and if he hadn't culled out a corner of her space to use as his makeshift office, he would have only seen her for a few minutes at night before they tumbled into sleep.

Late that afternoon, he stood outside a hotel near Central Park South with Ivan waiting for the next contestant. He checked the info Jayne had sent him. Mikala Mason's demo had impressed him. Her range stretched several octaves and the way she'd torn up one of The Fury's newer songs, *Shredded Justice,* was too awesome to believe.

He needed a good audition to take his mind off of the stress of dealing with Owen, of Audrey working with Owen, and the fact there was nothing he could do about it. Owen was like a constant dark cloud hanging over his mood. Guard up, Luke couldn't relax.

"Luke?"

He glanced up at his name. A sleek blonde

approached wearing tons of makeup, spiked heels, and a hot pink dress that left little to the imagination.

"Mikala?" Just to be sure... The woman in the video demo hadn't been as groupie-esque as the one who stood before him.

"Hi." She extended her hand. "I'm so excited to meet you."

"It's nice to meet you too." He shook her hand, and jolted back when she captured him in an exuberant hug, enveloping him in a cloud of sugary sweet perfume. Patting her back, he eased away. "Ready for your audition?"

Her eyes sparkled. "I'm ready for *you*."

Behind her, Ivan coughed, but it sounded strangely like a laugh.

Luke gestured toward the hotel's double doors. "We've reserved a conference room. When we get in there, we'll start recording. Just be natural. No need for nerves."

As soon as they stepped into the hotel lobby, she pulled out her phone. "Can we take a selfie?"

Before he could agree, she'd leaned in close and held up her phone. That cotton candy perfume was already giving him a headache. One picture quickly became five before she deemed the last one acceptable.

He moved away, creating some space between them. Mere moments later, Mikala was plastered up against his side. "We could go to your hotel room. That's more personal than a conference room. I think I'd do better there." She grabbed his forearm while she talked.

He shifted away again. "All auditions are taking place in the same type of room. The acoustics need to be similar." He'd made that shit up, but the way she was looking at him raised a red flag.

Mikala laid her hand on his shoulder. "Rules, hmm? I suppose I understand. Maybe later." Her gaze darted to Ivan and then back again. "When we're alone."

Red flag, again. But surely she realized she was way too young for him. He didn't want to hurt her feelings or embarrass her, but he didn't want to encourage her either. "We won't be alone. Ivan's here for the duration. And so are the fans watching at home." He pointed to the camera and gently stepped away.

He barely gave Ivan a glance, more intent on keeping his arms and legs away from Mikala. She seemed part octopus. The sooner he finished the audition, the sooner he could get back to the hotel and check in with Audrey. Their quick kiss goodbye when he'd left the studio hadn't been nearly enough to satisfy him.

Mikala beamed a smile and then grabbed his hand. She clutched tight as they walked through the hallways toward the conference room, words tumbling out of her brightly painted lips. He was impressed with her knowledge of the band's history, and less enthused with the extent of her knowledge of his personal life.

Within moments, they were seated at a table in the center of the room. Rather than sitting across from him, Mikala moved her chair until they were side by side. "This is cozier."

Warning sirens buzzed in his head. As casually as he could, Luke shifted his chair a few inches away.

"Let's take another selfie." Phone in hand, Mikala bumped her chair until it met his. She tilted her head until it almost rested on his shoulder. "Smile."

Luke forced his cheeks to lift into a semblance of a smile, but from his view, it was more of a grimace. Beside him, Ivan stifled another laugh.

"There." Fingers flying fast over the keys, she typed and then held out the screen to show the picture posted on her media feed, captioned *Luke and me* with a little heart.

Shit. He edged away again. At this rate, he'd be in the next conference room before the audition even began. "Start the recording, Ivan."

"It's already rolling, boss."

At Ivan's word, Luke glanced into the camera. "Hey guys. Luke here. I'm with the second contestant in the New Band Contest. This is Mikala Mason."

"Thank you for making me feel so welcome, Luke." Her voice purred, dropping an octave and her hand touched his.

Again, shit. That warning siren buzzed louder.

He moved her hand off of his and reached for his bottle of water. "Your voice impressed everyone in the band. So, you've been singing for how many years?"

"Several." She fluffed her hair and then rested her elbow on the table, hand under her chin, and gazed at him. "You've been singing for several, too. Life on the road must get lonely."

He resisted the urge to press his fingers over the dull thudding in his temples. This pre-audition interview was a disaster, but it could be edited later. "Not really. I travel with three other guys, our band manager, the road crew, and occasionally a dog. If you'll please stand in the center of the room, we can get started."

"Sure." She swayed out of her chair like a stripper giving a lap dance and sauntered to the center of the room.

"Whenever you're ready." He set his phone on the table and tried to relax. "We'd like you to sing *Shredded Justice* again."

She opened her mouth and the off-key notes and wrong tone scraped along his skin like a bad itch.

Gaping at Ivan, Luke shook his head. "Something's not right."

"Sounds more like something is dying a slow and painful death."

Luke stood, motioning for Mikala to stop singing. "Hold up. What's going on with your voice?"

A blush touched her cheeks and she placed her hand on her hip and cocked it out to the side, posing as though she were celebrity at a red carpet event. "What do you mean?"

Okay—so no stories of strained vocal cords or anything to remotely explain the reason. The voice on the demo hadn't sounded auto-tuned... not that auto-tune could correct what he'd just heard. "Want to try again? You sound completely different."

She cleared her throat and belted out the chorus of the song. The screeching was bad enough to curdle his blood.

"Stop. Just stop." He waved his hands to silence her. "What the hell is going on here?"

"I wanted to meet you. My friend let me record her voice and use it for the audition. I lip-synched when I recorded my demo."

"Holy shit." Ivan's murmur mirrored Luke's thoughts, just before *what the fuck* broke in. "Are you kidding me? You and your friend cooked up a little scheme so you could meet me?"

Wearing a siren's smile, she sashayed toward the table. "I guess I was a little bad. Can you blame me?"

"Do you know how many hours of auditions we sat through? How many people we considered? And you faked it? Why take the opportunity away from someone else?"

Instead of answering him, she narrowed her eyes at Ivan. "Give us a minute."

"I'll grab a smoke." Ivan set the camera on the table and then exited the room.

As soon as they were alone, Mikala brushed her fingers up and down Luke's arm. "Let me make it up to you. Any way at all you want. I've been told I have many hidden talents." The red claws on her fingertips traced along the top of his thigh.

Enough. Luke shrugged away from her touch. "I'm involved with someone."

Green eyes narrowed into slits and then she gave him a seductive smile too precise to be anything but well-practiced. "But she's not here now."

"Let me be clear. I'm not available."

"None of the blogs or gossip sites mentioned anything about a woman in your life. No one in The Fury fan club knows anything about it. Who is she?" The mutinous glare on Mikala's face reminded him of a volcano ready to blow.

"She's everything to me. That's all you need to know."

"But I'm... I'm..." She thrust out her chest and tossed her hair. "I'm perfect for you. You'd see if you gave me a chance."

"You were here to audition. For the band. Not for any other role. And you fucking lied about it all." He raked a hand through his hair. Frustration mounted into a pounding in his blood. His headache intensified. "Did you think we wouldn't realize your voice didn't match the one in the video?"

"I thought you'd meet me and not care about anything else." She lifted her shoulders. "I'm better than whoever you're with."

"The woman I'm with is the only one for me. And you're disqualified from the competition."

Eyes spitting fire, Mikala pushed away from the table. "I'm not happy. Your new label will hear from me."

He refrained from rolling his eyes. His band mates wouldn't care. Then again, knowing the guys, they'd likely bust his balls about it. Whatever. "Go ahead. I'm in charge of complaints."

"You can go to hell." She grabbed her purse and stalked out of the room.

That hadn't gone well. Blowing out a breath, he picked up the camera and went in search of Ivan. The bastard had high-tailed it to the hotel bar. Luke shoved the camera into Ivan's gut. "Thanks for leaving me hanging, bud. I'll remember that on our next tour."

Ivan pointed to the screen. "I left it set on recording, genius. I figured she'd say more if I wasn't there. So you have it documented."

"In that case, I owe you a drink. And I think I'll join you. What a fucking day. Do me a favor and forward the un-cut video to the guys. They need to see it."

Humid air greeted him when he stepped outside an hour later, but he relished being free of the sticky sweet perfume cloud he'd been stuck in all day. He fired off a text to his band mates ranting about the Mikala mess, then sent a text to Audrey to check in on her and headed to the hotel, in need of a shower and a pain killer.

By the time he finished and had a clearer, pain-free head, she still hadn't responded. He checked through his messages and did another social media sweep. People were commenting on Mikala's pictures. He'd received notifications because she'd tagged him in every one. What a fucking waste of time that had been.

His phone lit up with a call from Brendan. Needing to vent, he answered. "Hey, did you see the video?"

"Dude. Only you would have this happen." Brendan chuckled and Luke could picture his gray eyes brimming with laughter.

"It's not funny."

"Nope. It was a waste of time, and you handled yourself better than I would have expected. But really, you're in charge of complaints for us? *You?* Our resident hot head? I laughed so hard at that part, I nearly snorted beer out of my nose."

For the first time in hours, Luke cracked a smile. "Okay, so maybe I wouldn't be the first choice there."

"Try the last." He laughed again. "It'll be good to see you, man. Landry will be here soon. Our flight is at the butt crack of dawn, so we'll be in New York late morning, your time."

"Cool. You guys are staying at my hotel, right?" He hoped so.

"Yeah. Irisa made all the arrangements. Zander and Jayne are coming in from Maine, and Irisa is flying out from LAX around the same time as Landry and me. I think we're all meeting you at Audrey's studio at noon."

They chatted for a few more minutes, until Landry had arrived and said his own hello. Bidding his friends goodbye, Luke sat in the utter silence of the room.

He needed Audrey.

Finally, his phone pinged with her response.

Sorry, was busy with show stuff. Just got into a cab now.

Good. He'd feel a lot better after holding her. Lying across his bed, he typed his reply.

Is it cool if I come over?

He threw clothes into his carry-on bag. Then her reply chimed.

No.

His lungs froze. They hadn't slept apart since he'd returned from Nashville. He could sleep alone, but preferred dropping off into dreams while wrapped in his dream come true. Especially after the day he'd had.

Then her message continued:

I'm on my way to you.

***

Audrey hoisted her tote bag higher on her shoulder and made her way through Luke's hotel. Knowing how late she'd be working, she'd packed a change of clothes that morning. Luke's hotel was closer to her studio than her apartment. Exhaustion and needing to see him had made the decision easy.

Three straight days of working with him at her studio, and four straight nights of unwinding with him at the end of her day, of sharing a glass of wine, of climbing onto soft sheets with him, and then sleeping tucked against him throughout the night, had created a routine she craved.

It had also stoked her desire for more.

She'd wanted to go slow. Baby steps. But every taste of him only increased her hunger.

Three years of thinking about him, of interactions, glances, and incidental touches, tacked on to the time they'd spent together since he'd arrived in the city, gave her a clear picture of who he was. Moving forward and taking things to another level was scary, but holding back and keeping things exactly as they were wouldn't ever get her—get them—to where she wanted to be.

Heart pounding a little harder, she knocked on his door.

It swung open and Luke waved her inside. A smile lifted his cheeks, but something deeper, relief, reflected in his eyes and echoed in her soul. After her long day, all she wanted was him.

Hair damp, wearing workout shorts and a baseball t-shirt, he looked nothing like the lead singer who entertained thousands and sold out stadiums. He looked like a regular guy—if anything about Luke could actually be regular. He plowed his hands into her hair, cupping her head, and brought his mouth down to brush teasing kisses against her lips. "I needed this. My night was crazy."

"What happened?" She set her bag on the floor and stroked her fingers along the lines of tension in his face.

"My fan audition turned into a shit storm. The girl used someone else's voice in the demo she submitted. Apparently, she thought this would be a good way to meet me. I'm so pissed. She seemed to think I'd be cool with the fact she wasted my time and the band's time. She can't sing at all. Instead of her wanting to be in the group, she wanted to be a groupie. She offered to keep me company tonight, if you know what I mean."

She drew back. "Excuse me?"

He lifted one of her hands and placed it on his shoulder, and then wrapped his arms around her waist. "I put on the brakes, but she wasn't too happy."

"I can imagine..." Possessiveness snaked

through her as she pictured the woman putting moves on *her* man.

"All I wanted to do was get back to you. How was the rest of your day?"

"Long. Busy. Oh, and I pulled together a few things for you and the guys to wear on the show. Irisa called me a few hours ago and said everyone is flying in on Friday morning, and can stop by my studio around lunchtime."

"Yeah, Brendan confirmed those plans when I spoke with him earlier. They're all staying here at the hotel, too. I think she's doing that because both Zander and Brendan tend to lose track of time. Jett's show is live, so we can't be late."

"It'll be good for you to have some company and take a breather from the Furious Records project for a few days. But if the guys want to discuss things, just let me know."

He drew her further into the room and set her tote bag next to his luggage. "Your focus for the next few days is your fashion show. I'm grateful for all the time you've been sinking in to my project on top of your busy schedule, but I'll sure as hell like it better when you're not working fourteen hour days."

"Me too. I'll be taking some vacation time after the show is over." She wandered to the window. Fifteen stories below, the city pulsed to its own beat. "My parents want to see me for a few days. But maybe after that we could get out of the city for a weekend?"

"I like that idea." He sidled up behind her and wrapped his arms around her waist, nuzzling his face into her neck. "How's the west coast sound?

You can join me for both the fan audition in L.A., then the party in Vegas, and then after that, we can unwind at my place in Cali."

"You said you live near the beach, right?" She stepped out of her shoes.

"Very near." Luke tightened his hold, drawing her back against his chest. "I forget how small you are."

"I'm not that short."

"Not short. Delicate. And perfect. Perfect for me." Warm lips pressed the sensitive spot by her ear, then traveled along the slope of her neck.

Letting out a sigh, she reached for him and tangled her hand in his hair.

His hands roamed a slow journey from her waist to her breasts. When he cupped her, her head fell back onto his shoulder. His hands, lips, the slight scrape of his beard, and the hardness of his body sent her on sensation overload.

She tugged his head until his mouth latched onto hers. He tasted of mint, mixed with the cinnamon tea she'd had at the studio. She turned in his arms, angling for a more thorough taste.

Luke's fingers played with the cap sleeves of her shirt, then traced along the collar, then stroked their way down to the hem. "Too much material. I want to touch you."

"Please." After all the time that had passed, after all the imagining of her hands on him and his hands on her... finally. Finally. This was happening.

One by one, he popped the buttons open, then pushed the shirt off her shoulders. It caught at her hands and then fell to the floor.

"Gorgeous, Sunshine. You know that?" His appreciative smile accompanied his touch. Large hands molded her through the yellow satin bra. He kissed a line from her lips to the swell of her breasts, then closed his mouth over one peak while his fingers tightened on the other.

"Luke." Hands in his hair, she held him tighter to her, sighing when he pulled away the material and repeated his exploration with his mouth.

"I need to touch you, too." Her hands tugged at his shirt. Each inch revealed another section of defined abs, sculpted pecs, and the flexing muscles in his arms. He yanked the shirt over his head and tossed it toward the chair and then sucked in a breath when her hands raked over his skin. Desire ran through her, clean and strong and stoking the need for *more*. She couldn't touch him enough— slow sweeps down his arms, feather-light strokes along his back, and then grazing her nails over his stomach.

He reached for her, then dropped his hands to his sides. "I know we said baby steps. If I touch you any more, I'm not going to be able to stop."

Touching him felt too good. Being touched by him felt amazing. "I don't want to stop."

His eyes heated, grew hungry, and he traced his fingertips over her face. "Do you know why I call you *Sunshine*?"

She shook her head.

Luke smiled. "The first time we met, the day had been gray and overcast. And then I arrived for the photo shoot. And when I locked eyes with you, the sun came out, brilliant sunlight spotlighting you.

The sky cleared, and we touched hands, and something deep inside me brightened, too."

The threat of tears stung her eyes. "That's the most beautiful thing anyone has ever said to me."

"I just wanted you to know that before we go any further."

She stretched up to kiss him. "I haven't been the same either." With her hands on his waistband, she tugged him closer and worked the top button free.

Luke followed suit, finding the side zipper on her skirt. The skirt caught on her hips for a moment, then fluttered to the floor.

Gaze on his, Audrey gently tugged his zipper over the bulge in his jeans. His eyes closed when she parted the fabric and closed her hand over him. Breath hissed through his teeth and he rested his forehead against hers. "Sunshine..."

After a long moment, he eased out of her hold and dropped to his knees. Breath feathering over her stomach, he roamed lowered. Strong hands grazed over her hips and to the back of her thighs. He tugged the yellow lace at her hip lower and proceeded to drive her crazy with teases of his teeth and tongue.

"We should move to the bed." The words barely escaped her mouth before he swept her up in his arms and carried her over.

He tossed the blanket back and let her slide onto the soft white sheets first. The mattress dipped as he climbed in and knelt between her legs. He ran his hands from her calves to her thighs, then teased his way up her torso in deliberate strokes. When they were lined up, lips to lips and eyes to eyes, he eased his way inside.

Her breath caught and Luke groaned. He kissed her, thrusts of tongue mimicking the slow, seductive rocking of his hips. Audrey gripped his back and lifted into him, seeking him when he retreated. This wasn't just sex—this was sex with Luke. The difference was enough to overwhelm her. Everything intensified. And suddenly, she was flying high, swamped in pleasure as Luke increased his pace and then stiffened with a harsh groan of her name.

She brushed his hair off of his forehead and kissed him, lingering over his taste as her body calmed.

Luke lifted off of her and tugged the cover from the foot of the bed. He pulled it over them and lay on his side, facing her. "That was worth waiting for."

His lips met hers again, soft and romantic, stopping only for breaths, then coming together again.

Everything they'd said to each other, everything she'd felt, solidified that her decision to move forward had been the right one.

"Yes," she panted sweetly. "It was. But I won't make us wait as long for round two."

"Really?" He grinned and lowered his face to hers. "How long this time?"

"Depends on you," she whispered against his lips right before he sank in for a breath stealing kiss.

CHAPTER EIGHT

Luke sat in a soft leather chair in the front room of Audrey's studio. The guys were due to arrive any minute to pick out clothes for Jett's show. Sending out a reminder to the fans about the band's appearance on the show, he caught himself whistling again and glanced at the hallway, hoping Renee and Audrey hadn't heard.

Waking up wrapped in Audrey that morning had been the best feeling in the world. The sex had been incredible, but then again he'd expected it to be because it was with Audrey. The dark cave of drawn shades and curtains in his hotel room were a far cry from the white walls, big windows, and blinding light that poured into Audrey's apartment in the mornings. He definitely preferred her space, and how the light shined on her face, hair, and curves, but in his room she was in shadows and he wanted their relationship in the light. Hopefully, they would be sleeping there tonight.

He sipped his coffee and glanced at his watch. Now that he'd had a taste of what life was like with Audrey in it, he wanted more. Even after their night together, he was afraid of pushing too hard or too fast. Luke knew he didn't possess much restraint, but for her, he'd try his damnedest.

"Hey, there he is." Brendan's voice pulled him from his thoughts. The drummer walked in, grinning, arms stretched wide. He hugged Luke hard.

Zander, Jayne, Landry, and Irisa trooped into the room. It hadn't been too long since he'd seen his friends, but damn, he'd missed them. Hugs and greetings were exchanged, loud enough to draw out Audrey and Renee from the back room. And then the introductions and reunions began all over again.

Luke's heart beat uncomfortably in his chest when Audrey met Jayne. They shared certain personality traits, and the similarities had been too much for him to handle when he'd thought he'd lost Audrey all those months ago. Suffering hadn't made him kind back then. Luckily, Jayne didn't hold a grudge. Neither did Zander. But Luke still felt bad about it.

Audrey and Jayne hit it off immediately and continued to chat, laughing and smiling in instant friendship.

Zander joined him on the other side of the room. "You were right about their voices being similar."

"Told you." His guilt eased when Zander dropped his arm around his shoulder.

"You okay? You're quiet. Things good with Audrey?"

"I think they're moving in the right direction. But I'm—"

"Still afraid you might fuck it up?"

"Yeah."

"You probably will, but then again we all do.

Just be honest with her. That's the best thing. But I can see she makes you happy. She looks happy too."

Hopefully, he made her happy. He followed the rest of the guys into the back room. A whirlwind of clothes made their way to him. He trusted Audrey's taste, and she knew what looked best on him, so he didn't argue. The jeans, gray shirt, jacket and boots worked for him. The other guys weren't picky either, but Landry refused to trade his beat up leather jacket for the new jacket in Renee's hands.

While the bassist debated the virtues of his fake leather over the real thing, Luke pulled Audrey aside. "You're coming to the show, right?" He posed the question partly to feel out her preference for sleeping that night, but he genuinely wanted her in the audience.

"Absolutely. I'm excited to see you in action."

"Awesome." He was more than a little excited she'd agreed to be there. But then again, she could be the only person in attendance and he'd be happy. "We wanted to announce you as our designer for everything, too. We can all grab something to eat afterward. And then maybe I can head home with you."

"I have to get up ridiculously early tomorrow to prep things for the show. I won't be much company tonight."

"I don't mind. We don't have to do anything— just go home and sleep. And I'll help out with whatever you need tomorrow."

"You won't mind hauling boxes and helping set up? I mean, there will be a crew too, but, really, you'd help?"

"Without complaining. And I'll bring the coffee."

A smile bloomed across her face and eased the tension in his gut. "You're hired."

Hours later, the band walked onto the set of *Hard and Heavy Live*. Luke waved to the crowd, and then winked at Audrey in the audience, seated between Irisa and Jayne.

After Jett did his set up and introduced the band, he gestured to Luke's outfit. "I'm sorry, I can't just let this slide by. Your appearance today is a big step up from the last time I saw you."

The giant screen behind them showed side by side pictures of Luke. Leather jacket, shirt and jeans in the live shot and a picture of him in an ancient tee and ripped jeans from the time he'd met Jett for an impromptu lunch. The audience laughed and catcalled his improved look.

Laughing, Luke shrugged. "What can I say? The best designer in the business put this together for me, so give Audrey Pierce all the credit. All of us guys are wearing her label tonight, and she's the artist who created our new label's logo."

Jett grinned. "You two were in your own little world when I stopped by the green room to say hi before the show. Tell me, is it serious with Audrey? If it is, you just broke the hearts of half your female fans."

The camera panned to Audrey. Her eyes widened, her mouth gaped, and a deep pink blush crept over her neck and cheeks.

What the hell? Luke blinked. Jett was supposed to talk about their new label and the band's contest, not question him on his love life. Part of him wanted to keep Audrey all to himself. The rest of him wanted to stake his claim.

Brendan waved his hand. "Hold up there, Jett. I wouldn't say Luke has half the fans' hearts. Maybe a quarter. The rest of us guys have fans, too. Am I right?" He grinned at the audience and beckoned for them to make some noise. Cheers resounded.

Jett smiled as the camera again came to a rest on Audrey. "I didn't mean to put you on the spot. Gang, let's give Audrey a round of applause for being a good sport."

Fuck it. Luke stood. Keeping his gaze on Audrey's, he strolled to her seat. Blue eyes full of questions, she mouthed *what*. He grasped her hand and gently pulled until she stood by his side.

"What are you doing?" Her whisper ghosted his cheek. Her hand trembled in his and Luke squeezed to reassure her.

"Clearing up any doubts about what I want." He threaded his hand in her hair and lowered his mouth to brush against her petal-soft lips.

A soft gasp, and then she opened for him, allowing him to take the kiss deeper. Like a drug, she flooded his system. Cheers from the crowd accompanied whistles and cat-calls. Pulling away from her required more effort than he'd expected.

With his arm around her waist, he turned toward the stage. "Does that answer your question?"

More cheers rose up around them and Jett waved to quiet them down.

Audrey's hand lay against his chest. Luke smiled down at her. "See you after the show, Sunshine." He couldn't help taking another taste, and then made his way back to his seat.

"Dude." Brendan shook his head, grinning. "Nice job."

He shrugged, then accepted a slap on the back from Zander.

Jett directed the questions and conversation back to the scheduled topics. Until he mentioned Zander's recent engagement to Jayne. As with Audrey, the camera panned to Jayne. Her hand played with the heart pendant necklace she always wore.

Zander tapped Luke's shoulder as he stood. "Can't have my singer outdo me." He made his way into the audience and kissed Jayne, adding in an elaborate dip.

After the audience quieted and Zander returned to his seat, Jett raised his brows. "So all is right in The Fury's world?"

"It's fucking awesome." Luke shifted as the phone in his pocket buzzed. Probably fans responding to the live show. "We're launching our label, Furious Records, and we're exciting to be auditioning fans to form our label's first group."

Furious Records' logo, bold white letters on a black square appeared on the screen. Jett gave it an approving nod. "The logo rocks. And you guys are probably loving that you'll retain full control this way."

"You trying to say we have a problem dealing with authority?" Luke quirked his brow and the audience laughed.

"Any idea when you'll start recording again?"

Zander spoke for the group, "We just started decompressing from the non-stop action that we kept up for years, plus we're devoting all our time to the fan auditions and gearing up for the launch party in a few weeks, where we'll announce the new band winners. So give us at least this summer, man."

"Can I get you on record saying you're not breaking up? We've had so many people write in, asking that question, in prep for tonight's show."

"We're not breaking up." Luke sighed. He couldn't get angry, he knew Jett wanted to ask the question to quiet the rumor mill. "We love our music and our fans too much to stop. Creating Furious Records is our promise to them and our commitment to each other."

"And we look forward to hearing the new band perform live, right here on our stage two weeks after their launch party." Jett smiled at the camera, then turned to face the band. "Since the fans will have to wait a bit to hear you play together again, how about you guys give us a song here?"

Luke locked eyes with Audrey. It wasn't the song he and the guys had practiced backstage, but he knew exactly what he wanted to do.

***

The band stood up from the chairs and headed toward the instruments set up in the left side of the set. Audrey turned to Irisa. "What song are they going to play?"

"Beats me. They rehearsed a few today, including covers of some other bands. So I have no idea."

Music started, but it wasn't the hard and heavy beats the guys were known for. Luke leaned into the microphone. "This one's for Audrey."

It was slower, less aggressive, and vaguely familiar. But she couldn't place it. When Luke crooned out the first line, she knew. One of the love songs he'd been singing every morning while in the shower. The decades' old song made modern and tough enough for a rock band with faster beats and heavy guitars and Luke almost growling the lyrics.

Touched, she grinned at him and then admired an artist in action. He sang with his whole body. And his facial expressions mirrored the words he sang and the feelings invoked. He caught her gaze a few times and winked.

A woman behind her murmured, "Lucky bitch."

Surprise shot through her. Audrey glanced at Jayne and Irisa. From their shocked and annoyed expressions, they'd heard the woman. Thoughts tumbled—should she ignore it, turn around and say something, or laugh it off?

Irisa nudged her and her head shook slightly. Let it go. But she didn't want to be a doormat. Heart beating fast, she turned. Two women sat behind her. Both wore The Fury t-shirts. One smirked at her while the other eyed her with cool disinterest.

Saying something now wouldn't solve anything and would only cause a scene. She faced forward. If she had to bet, she'd put money on the smirker. But then again, the other woman had *Luke* tattooed on her arm. The incident tinged her enjoyment of Luke's gift to her, but then the band launched into one of their high octane numbers, and the entire crowd was on their feet. Being upset about a tiny comment she wasn't entirely sure was directed at her didn't make much sense when she had a new friend in Jayne, a reliable friend in Irisa, and the company of an entertaining group of guys. And, most of all, when she had Luke.

The next afternoon, controlled chaos reigned at the venue she'd rented out for the show. Instead of a regular fashion show, the models would begin by walking across a stage set up like a typical rock concert, with guitars and a drum kit, while lights flashed in the background. They'd then move to a low catwalk that would bring them out into the "pit". Afterward, more of a party atmosphere would take over, with models walking around wearing the designs, mingling with the attendees. Food, drink, music, and hopefully, lots of sales and new clients.

Audrey rushed between checking on progress with the models getting dressed, hair and make-up, and last-minute chats with the venue manager. Her nerves increased with each passing minute. In addition to the bands she'd invited, other band managers, rock news bloggers and reporters, fashion bloggers, and record company representatives would also be in attendance. And of course, the director of the domestic violence program. Now was not the time for anything to go wrong.

Renee flagged her down. "Jacob can't go on. He just called me. He's home, and sick as a dog. Stomach bug."

"Ugh. Seriously? Now?" She glanced at her list, hoping a last-minute replacement would appear.

Luke approached her. He'd been a huge help all day long, doing anything that needed to be done. "Need anything else from me? If not, I'll go join the guys out front."

"One of my models got sick." She bit her lip and looked him up and down. Different coloring than Jacob, but a similar enough build. "You guys are about the same size. It could work..."

"You want me to walk down the runway?" He shook his head and laughed. "I'm not a model."

"Please? You'd be perfect. And I need you. I'm already short a few guys. I need to balance it out."

"I can't say no to you, not when you look at me like that..." He gave her a begrudging smile. "All right, I'll do it. But no makeup."

She threw her arms around him and squeezed him hard. "Thank you. I owe you."

He threaded his fingers in her hair and gently pulled until her lips met his. Soft, warm, and a hint of mint. His taste was already so familiar. His tongue traced the seam until her lips parted and he groaned as she brushed into his wet heat. Audrey's fingers teased the back of his neck and she snuggled closer.

A throat clearing behind her, followed by a tap on her shoulder, brought her back to reality.

Renee stood, hands on hips. "Clock's ticking, guys. Come on, Luke, I'll show you where you can change clothes."

He reluctantly loosened his hold on Audrey. "Man, the guys are going to have a field day with this..."

Audrey checked once again on the models' progress, fixed a last-minute stitch for Vanessa, and then answered a few questions from reporters.

Owen threaded his way toward her. Audrey immediately glanced around for Luke, relieved when she didn't see him. "Hi, are you looking for Vanessa? I think she's back in make-up."

"I wanted to talk to you."

"Oh? Is something wrong with the clothes you bought?" She'd spent a few hours with him earlier in the week, talking design, trying to find out what would suit him best. She'd found him to be smug about his band and vocal talents but he definitely seemed to care about Vanessa, and that counted for a lot.

He shook his head. "Clothes are fine. Great quality. Look, you seem nice enough but hanging around Luke is a mistake."

Taken aback, she blinked. "Luke may be a little gruff but he's a good guy."

"He's an asshole. A failure. And failing is contagious."

She didn't appreciate him coming into her space and talking about Luke that way. Hands on her hips, she glared at him. "It's really none of your business. I can take care of myself."

Brow raised, he shrugged and then sneered. "Don't say I didn't warn you."

"I'm not going to listen to you insulting Luke.

You should probably take your seat out front. We're going to be starting soon." She felt a lot better when he walked away. Maybe his concern came from a good place, but neither he nor Luke were innocent in their feuding. He couldn't fault her man for everything.

As time ticked down, she directed people to scatter so the models could line up. She'd put Luke last in line to give him enough time to get ready.

The music began, a thundering beat to set the tone. One by one, the models processed across the stage, then down the runway in dramatic fashion.

Ready or not, the show had begun.

***

Luke waited at the side of the stage. Stage lights—fine. A crowd watching him—not a problem. But singing was one thing, walking a runway was another. As the other model came up the runway and exited stage-left, Audrey nudged his arm. "Now."

The spotlight rested on him. Luke walked across the low stage, then turned onto the catwalk. The runway was only a foot about the floor. He could step off it and walk right into the crowd. The music changed—his cue to stroll down. One foot, then the other. He didn't smile because models on the runway never smiled. Plus, he didn't belong there. He felt like an impostor, but he'd do anything for Audrey. Halfway down, he spotted his band sitting at the end. Zander, Brendan, and Landry all grinned, calling out suggestions and encouragement, and taking pictures.

His skin heated. Damn it. Scowling, he did his best to ignore his band.

When he reached them, Brendan jumped up and held up his phone. "You clean up nice, man. Take a pic with me? The fans will go nuts."

"Sit down." But he paused for a second to let Brendan get the shot he wanted. And then came the easy task of walking back. When he reached the edge of the stage, he turned and waited with the other models.

Audrey made her way across the stage, shining in a bronze dress sprinkled with sequins and a tiny, shrunken black leather jacket that fit her like a second skin. She didn't walk the runway, but stood in the center of the stage. Applause burst in waves from the crowd, and Luke joined in. He followed the other models as they formed a line behind her across the stage. Pride for her filled him to bursting.

And then, the runway portion and his brief career as a model were over.

Backstage again, he waited as she thanked each model individually. Then she turned to him and slipped her arms around his waist. "You did a great job. Thank you so much for filling in."

"Anything for you." He bent to kiss her. "I'm so proud of you."

Someone called her name from across the room. She drew back. "I have to go."

"Have fun, work that room. I'll find you after the party." He let her go and went in search of his band mates.

Music flowed and lights shimmered, wait staff

worked the room with champagne and food, and the models mingled with the attendees. People stood in small clusters, smiling, talking, drinking, eating, and best of all, complimenting Audrey's clothes.

Zander and the guys stood by the stage. Luke dodged a few people admiring one of the models and came face to face with Owen.

Shit. He'd managed to avoid the jerk earlier and had hoped to get through the day without crossing paths.

"Good for you, finding a fall back career." Owen set his empty glass on a passing waiter's tray.

Luke's promise to Audrey echoed in his head. He would *not* get sucked in. "Fuck off."

"You'll need a new career, after the way you screwed up your last tour. That arrest for drinking while boating—which I found funny as hell, by the way. Then the bar fight, and then you no-showing to that concert. Class act stuff. I shared those headlines around as much as I could. Did you notice that? Just like I'll share the next one. Because there will be a next one. Face it, you're a fuck up, and you're going to fuck up this Furious Records idea too. I can't wait to see you fail."

Don't give him the satisfaction... Luke crossed his arms over his chest. If they were crossed, he couldn't punch the bastard. "Do you spend all your time focusing on me? I'm flattered."

Eyes narrowed, Owen stepped into Luke's space. "Don't be."

"Back off, man."

"You going to make me?"

Hands itching to fight, anger pounding in his

veins, Luke turned away. To his right, Vanessa strode toward them, probably rushing to run interference. She stepped into a small puddle of spilled wine on the floor. Her foot slipped forward and her body swayed backward and her eyes went wide.

"Hey." Luke moved fast, grabbing her arms. Her hands landed on his shoulders, pulling at the fabric.

Once he'd righted her, something hard slammed into the center of his back. "Keep your hands off her."

Pain bloomed and radiated to his arms. Luke spun to face Owen. "Maybe if you'd been paying more attention to her, I wouldn't have had to save her."

"Fuck you." Owen's fist flew forward, heading for Luke's face.

Luke threw up his arm to block it, and then countered with a left hook. "Asshole."

Owen's head snapped back, and then he launched at Luke, grabbed him by the waist and tackled him. Concrete slammed into his back, winding him. Owen's fist connected with his jaw. Luke's teeth clacked together. Hopefully, it wasn't broken. He grappled with him, throwing his full weight, and succeeded in reversing their positions. He landed a few quick jabs to Owen's ribs.

Footsteps and shots echoed around them.

"Stop it!"

"Luke!"

Anger burned through his veins. Goddamn Owen. He'd been waiting for an opportunity to smash his face for years. They rolled around on the floor. Owen sputtered curses as he landed blows, blood dripping from his nose. Luke's jaw ached, his hand hurt, and breath burned in and out of his lungs, but he shoved back hard, giving as good as he got.

Strong hands grabbed his shoulders and hauled him away from Owen.

"What the hell?" He jerked his head around. Zander and Brendan held him in a tight grip.

A few feet away, Landry and a security guard had a similar grip on Owen's shoulders.

Zander leaned in. "You okay? What the hell happened?"

The silence blanketing the room was deafening. Then the click of heels sounded. A single pair, making their way in his direction.

Luke turned toward the sound.

Audrey.

And she looked as upset as a drummer who'd just had his sticks broken.

CHAPTER NINE

Audrey stood between Luke and Owen. Noise from their altercation had pulled her away from a discussion about creating designs for a new all-woman rock band. When she'd heard the first crash, she'd thought someone had fallen. When she'd heard the shouts and scuffling and Luke and Owen snarling at each other, dread and worry had taken hold, until anger had overtaken everything.

Aware of every eye in the place focused on her, she squeezed her fists until her nails threatened to bite into her palms. The pain helped her keep her voice even. "Luke and Owen, let's clear this matter up in the dressing room. Everyone, please enjoy the party. Fresh champagne will be circulating shortly."

Music resumed and Renee gave her a nod as she passed. "I'll handle the crowd out here, boss."

In the dressing room, Audrey whirled to face Luke, supported by Zander and Brendan, and Owen, still restrained by Landry and the security guard. Vanessa, Irisa, and Jayne filed in behind.

"You have two seconds to tell me what the hell happened out there."

"He touched my girl." Owen shrugged away from his restraints, but Landry, Zander, and Brendan still blocked his access to Luke.

The muscles in Luke's arms tightened like he anticipated an attack. "Her *arms*. Preventing her from falling. And you know that's true."

"Luke's right." Vanessa's soft voice was a huge contrast to the booming argument.

"And that turned into you beating each other out there?" Audrey shook her head. "I really don't want to hear any more. Owen, I think it's best if you leave. Vanessa, thank you for working today's show. You don't have to stick around until the end."

Owen pushed his way out of the room, flipping off Luke one last time. Vanessa made quiet apologies and exited behind him. The security guard followed, murmuring he'd watch over the pair until they vacated the building.

Audrey took in Luke's disheveled state. He had red marks on his face, Owen's blood on his shirt, and a rip at the knee of his left pant leg. "And you. What the hell? Can't you control your temper? You don't settle arguments that way."

Rubbing his jaw, Luke glared at the door Owen had exited. "He started it."

"Oh for—" She pushed her hair out of her face. "Are you kidding me? 'He started it?' This isn't a playground fight. This is my business, my livelihood, and you ruined my show. I don't care what kind of history you guys have. You've embarrassed me in front of my current clients, possible future clients, and the media."

His shoulders lifted and then he glanced at the ground for a moment before rubbing his hand over his neck. "I'm sorry."

"You promised me." The words whispered out,

as shaky as her hold on her tears. She'd told him how important the show was to her. "You promised you would get along."

"Sunshine, listen—"

"Please leave." She couldn't talk to him. Not now, not here. Too many emotions swirled and too many people hovered. She would not create another scene.

"Audrey."

She held up her hand, held him away. "Leave. I really can't talk to you now. I don't want to say something I'll end up regretting."

"But—"

Something inside was threatening to shake loose. She'd either burst into tears or bust out a punch of her own. Her muscles shook with the effort to control herself. "Luke, I really need you to leave me alone."

Brendan placed his hand on Luke's shoulder. "Come on, bud. Let's go."

Zander flanked his other side, gently easing him away. "Let's get you back to the hotel and cleaned up."

Landry joined them. "You need ice and pain relievers. You're going to feel like hell in the morning."

When the door closed behind Landry, Audrey turned away, breathing deep. Hurt, anger, embarrassment, and annoyance fought for dominance.

"What can we do to help?" Irisa stepped closer, but still kept some distance.

"I need to go out there and mingle and get

people to talk about the clothes." Not at all what she felt like doing. She could barely wrap her head around what had happened.

Irisa closed the distance between them and hugged her. "It'll be fine. We'll help. I've been promoting your clothes for years. Jayne has worked with bands that have worked with you, too. She can attest for how amazing the clothes look on stage."

"True." Jayne smiled and walked toward the door. "Now let's sell those clothes."

Two hours later, the party had ended, the models had gone home, and Audrey sat in her studio with Renee, Irisa, and Jayne. "They ruined my show. All anyone wanted to talk about was the two of them."

Renee glanced up from rearranging some fabric swatches. "There's no such thing as bad publicity."

"Really? Because the domestic violence program's director didn't seem too thrilled with what had happened. She said I'll hear from her by Monday. I have a feeling I can kiss that partnership goodbye."

"You don't know that yet." Renee was determined to be an optimist.

"I think so when people are mostly going to be talking about how two famous rockers turned my show into their own boxing ring. Screw the clothes, let's focus on the fact that these two idiots have a new item to add to their feud." Seething, Audrey scrolled through mentions of the fight from several media outlets. "See? It's already happening that way. And the fact that I'm involved with one of them? That my own boyfriend doesn't even respect my wishes enough to control himself?"

"That's the real reason you're angry." Irisa put her hand on her shoulder. "I love Luke like he's my own brother. There have been times he's done things that make me want to throttle him, but underneath it all, he really is a good guy."

"He wouldn't set out to deliberately hurt you either." Jayne played with the heart-shaped pendant dangling from her necklace. "I think you'll end up getting more business. Most people who attended will feel sympathy for you because of it, and may double the number of pieces they were planning on purchasing. And on that note, there are three designs I saw that I'd like to buy for myself, and four more that I think would look amazing on Zander."

"Oh," Renee waved her hand. "I want that light pink dress with the leather and studs."

"Me too," Irisa chimed in. "And I want you to custom-make Dom's and the groomsmen tuxes for the wedding. You can do that, can't you?"

Her mood lightened and Audrey couldn't fight the beginning of a smile. "Guys, how am I supposed to stay angry when you're being so nice to me?"

"You're not." Renee tapped her on the shoulder. "Come on, let's go out and celebrate a successful show."

"Successful?"

"Okay, let's drink wine and go dancing and forget about our men."

"I'm in." But it would take a hell of a lot of wine and a hell of a lot of dancing to make her forget.

***

After a restless night in his lonely hotel bed with a bottle of pain reliever and guilt as his companion, Luke trudged down to the hotel's restaurant for breakfast with the band. The guys had hung out with him for most of the night, keeping him calm enough that he hadn't gone looking for Owen or done anything else stupid, and keeping his spirits from dropping too far into black. He needed to talk to Audrey, had taken his phone out several times to call her, but her request to be left alone had stopped him from dialing every time.

Not in the mood to talk to anyone else, he pulled his baseball cap low and entered the restaurant. The band crowded around one round table in a sectioned-off nook. Grateful for the privacy, he joined them. Landry and Brendan sprawled on one side of the table, with Irisa, Zander, and Jayne on the other.

He nodded at their greetings and eased his body into the open chair between Brendan and Jayne. His back, knee, and side exploded in pain. Goddamn Owen.

His throbbing muscles protested as he reached for the pot of coffee at the center of the table. Knuckles swollen, he couldn't even grip the handle. "Fuck it," he muttered.

"Let me," Jayne said, taking pity on him and pouring the steaming liquid into his cup.

"Thank you." His jaw hurt, but he could talk without too much soreness and his beard mostly hid the large bruise blooming there.

She set the creamer and sugar by his cup. "How are you feeling today?"

"Like I was in a fight."

Brendan passed him platters of eggs, toast, and bacon. "You look like you lost it, too."

"Funny." He smirked and slid a portion of the food onto his plate. It would probably taste like chalk, given his mood, but he'd eat.

"Actually, it's not." Irisa set down her phone. Her lips pressed together and she pinched the bridge of her nose. Her soft sigh cut into him. "Your scuffle went viral. I've received tons of calls and emails. My phone has been burning up since it happened."

His too. He closed his eyes for a moment, agonized to become her problem child once again. "I'm sorry. Send them my way. It's my fault, so I'll deal with it."

"No. That's my job. But you can make a public statement if you'd like. In fact, you should. We can work on it after breakfast."

"Thanks. Without you, I'd fuck up the apology, too." His glanced back and forth between Irisa and Jayne. "How was Audrey last night?"

"Upset."

"Angry."

Guilt tripled. All through the night, he'd berated himself for letting himself be goaded. He needed to make it right. "I know I screwed up. Goddamn Owen. Once he hit me, I couldn't hold back. The one thing she asked me to do, and I couldn't fucking keep it together for her."

Jayne's hand covered his. "Throwing a punch after he threw one at you is reflex. You were protecting yourself. Cut yourself some slack."

"You're too nice to me sometimes."

"And you're being a little too hard on yourself. People make mistakes. You'll make it right."

Jayne was one of the most forgiving people he knew. Even after all that had happened between them. He swallowed against the thickness in his throat, gently squeezed her hand, and leaned into the table to catch Zander's gaze. "You really lucked out with Jayne."

"I know." Zander wrapped his arm around his fiancée's shoulders. "You haven't spoken to Audrey yet?"

"Not since she told me to leave her alone. Once my public apology is live, I'll make a private one... if she's willing to hear me out."

"A little groveling is good for the soul," Jayne reminded him.

He nodded. "It might take more than that."

Two hours later, he stood on the front steps of Audrey's building. When she answered the buzzer, he wished there were a camera so he could see her. Especially if he ended up apologizing from the stoop. "It's me. Can I come up?"

No response. Was she ignoring him or coming down to chew him out? He reached for the buzzer again as the outer door unlocked. The knot in his stomach eased then tightened again. He still had to apologize and she still could throw him out at the end of it. The short climb to her floor seemed to double in length.

Before he could knock, her door opened. He stepped forward and stuck his foot in the threshold in case she tried to slam it in his face.

Red-rimmed, puffy eyes met his. A gray tank top and black yoga pants hugged her curvy form. She wore no makeup, no jewelry, and no welcoming smile. The down-turn of her lips crushed him. He'd done that to her. He rolled his shoulders in prep for the battle that lay ahead. "I'm sorry. I keep screwing up with you."

Her gaze dropped to the bouquet of yellow gerbera daisies in his hand.

"Here." He held them out. "They reminded me of you."

"They're pretty." She brushed her finger over a petal but made no move to take them from his hand.

She was so listless. Panic spanned out from his core. He needed a reaction from her—anything, even fighting with him. He blurted out, "Can I come in?"

She squared her shoulders, nodded, and opened the door wide enough for him to enter.

He laid the blooms on the coffee table, then shoved his hands in his back pockets and wandered further into the room. The bed, draped in the soft, romantic curtain, teased at something he might never have again. Would she tell him they were through? He breathed in deep, once, twice, and then turned to face her. "I tried yesterday. Really, I did. Even when he started provoking me, I didn't take the bait. But when he threw that punch... well, instinct kicked in. All the history and bad blood between us clouded my better judgment."

Hands clasped, she stood by the couch. "If I'd realized the extent of how much you guys dislike each other, I would've asked you to stay away from the show."

"No. That's not fair. I'm the man in your life, not Owen. And I wanted to be there. With you. For you. I don't want you to shut me out of things. Owen and I are going to run into each other, that can't be helped."

"But you can't come to blows anymore either."

"I know."

"You could've been seriously hurt."

"I know," he said again. "But the worst part is I hurt you. I let you down. I fucked up and I'm sorry."

"Apology accepted." Her eyes softened enough for him to see forgiveness shining through the shield, but the stiff way she held her body signaled things weren't entirely smoothed over.

Shifting his stance, he waited for more. "But?"

A sigh escaped her lips. She raked her hand through her hair and sank onto the arm of the couch. Her fingers plucked at the edge of a throw pillow. "But I'm still upset, okay? The fight is all anyone is talking about. You and Owen and your ridiculous feud, not the designs. That tells me one of two things. Either they're ignoring the clothes completely because a brawl between two rock stars is far more interesting. Or, now that Rob is no longer in the picture, my supporters no longer care to stick around. Both scenarios suck. My phone's ringing, but instead of buyers, it's reporters hoping for a good sound bite."

He'd do anything to change what happened, to

replace her wounded expression with a smile of love. "I'm sorry my fight is overshadowing your show. Before the fight, the attendees were talking about how much they loved the designs, so I'm sure orders will be coming in soon. And Rob's backing may have gotten the ball rolling a few years ago, but you created your success."

"We'll see."

"What about the partnership with the domestic violence program? Did you talk to the program director last night?"

The corners of her mouth turned down again. "She called with her decision this morning. The fight was a big factor in her reason for turning me down. You were the other."

"Me?"

"In the last few months, you've been in a few bar fights that have made the news. Obviously, violence is a problem for them. They don't condone it, and you're attached to too much of it. She said she couldn't let the partnership go through when I'm attached to someone with such strong tendencies toward violence. They're going with another designer."

"Shit. Sunshine, I'm so sorry." He dropped to his knees in front of her and grasped her hands in his.

She shrugged, but her face crumpled and the muscles in her throat worked. "It's... okay, I guess." Her teeth bit into her lip and her breath came in shallow rises. When the first tear tracked down her cheek, he hauled her into his arms.

Wanting to kick his own ass for being the cause

of her tears, he sat on the couch, holding her, rubbing her back while her tears soaked into his shirt. "I'm sorry. I'm sorry. I know how much that meant to you."

Shoulders shaking, she hiccupped and gasped out breaths. Finally, she raised her head and swiped her hands over her cheeks. "I didn't mean to break down. I'm sorry."

"Don't ever apologize for showing me how you feel. I hate that I ruined this for you."

"It's all right. I know you didn't mean to." She offered him a watery smile.

He truly didn't deserve her. How could she forgive him for fucking up so badly? "I posted an apology right before I came over here. Irisa sent it out as a press release. I'd like you to take a look at it."

She moved to sit on the cushion beside him and opened her laptop on the coffee table. Luke rubbed at the discomfort in his gut. His apology was posted on his personal pages, the band's pages, and the band's website.

I apologize for my actions during the incident at Audrey Pierce's fashion show. I created a distraction and removed the focus from this incredibly talented designer and her new collection. If you're a rocker, or want to dress like one, I encourage you to check out her clothes and jewelry.

"Thank you. I appreciate it. You didn't have to do that."

"Yes I did." He took a chance and laid his hand on her knee.

"Your hand is swollen." Soft fingertips brushed

the red skin. She lifted his hand to her lips and pressed a kiss to his knuckles.

He still felt bad about stealing her spotlight, and really bad for ruining her opportunity with the domestic violence program, but the knot in his stomach disappeared, the tightness in his shoulders eased, and the worry gripping his heart melted away. "My chin hurts too."

The corners of her mouth turned up in a smile. She leaned in and placed a soft kiss on his chin. "Your beard hides most of the redness there. When you left yesterday, I knew you were in pain. I wanted to punch Owen myself for hurting you."

"I'd pay to see that."

Her laugh touched off his own. Things were better. The guilt lingered, but he would do whatever he could to make it up to her. Maybe they could go to dinner or he could give her a massage or something as a start. "Want to get out of here for a bit?"

"Sure." She reached for the laptop, then pointed at the next picture on his page. "Oh hey, it's us."

He leaned in. Jett had posted the group picture, taken backstage after the show's taping. At center, Luke stood with his arms wrapped around Audrey. They were laughing along with the rest of the band and Irisa and Jayne as they all crowded together to fit in the shot. "That's a great picture."

"It received lot of comments." She stiffened and he glanced at the feed.

01_Fury_Fan: Who is the woman Luke is hugging?

The-Fury-Rules: Her name is Audrey. He said

113

on the show that they are dating, and he kissed her in front of everyone there.

01_Fury_Fan: Nooooooooo! He's mine!!!!

Luke_Is_My_Hero: I just looked her up. She's a NYC fashion designer for rock bands. She was a big fat nobody before dating rock god Rob Hawke.

The-Fury-Rules: Everyone knows when Rob Hawke backs something, it becomes a success. And she was so much younger than him, fourteen years. I bet I can figure out the attraction for both of them there... She used Rob to break into the music world.

The-Fury-4-Ever: Sounds like she slept her way to fame. Typical. What a skank.

Luke_Is_My_Hero: It looks like they broke up a few months ago. Maybe she used Rob up and needed fresh meat? The Fury have a huge and younger fan base. Poor Luke is going to get hurt.

01_Fury_Fan: She's using Luke to promote her brand. I can't stand girls like that. Luke is so perfect. He deserves so much better.

And it continued, on and on, comment after comment, fans weighing in on "the Audrey situation".

Luke blinked at the screen. The torrent of harsh comments continued to roll in.

What. The. Hell.

***

Mouth gaping open, Audrey stared at the comment feed. More and more messages appeared as people chimed in. Luke's fans were fiercely loyal and fiercely protective of him. Vicious comments had never happened when she'd been with Rob. At least, she'd never been aware of them. But this tidal wave of speculation and judgment was overwhelming. "They're wrong about everything other than the fact that I dated Rob."

"I know it, Sunshine. I know it." Luke's hand caressed her back in tight circles. His other hand curled to a fist on his thigh.

New comments popped up.

Mikala_Mason: I don't see why she's so great. She's not even pretty. And look at those thighs. He could do so much better.

Recognition dawned, even as her cheeks flushed and she contemplated her thighs. They'd always been her trouble spot. "She's the one who faked her audition demo so she could meet you, right?"

Luke turned the computer screen away. "Right. But don't listen to her. You're gorgeous. Every part of you. And I love your thighs."

His words were a balm but Audrey couldn't help pulling the screen back. The comment feed was like a car wreck—too tempting not to look.

Fury_Fan_4ever: Typical slut. He should dump that opportunistic leech—fast.

01_Fury_Fan: Seriously. Using first Rob, and now Luke to further her career. Luke should open his eyes.

Mikala_Mason: Poor Luke is clueless about her. He needs a real woman who can take care of him. Someone needs to help him wake up and realize what kind of person this fame-whore really is.

Fury_Fan_4ever: Or maybe someone else needs to come in and push her out of the picture...

Mikala_Mason: I would love to see that! This girl needs to go. She ruined my chance with him, so I HATE her!!!

The words cut deep. Audrey rubbed her hand over her chest. "Oh my goodness."

"That's enough of that." Luke closed the computer and put it out of reach. Aside from the clenching of his jaw and fists, he seemed calm. She'd expected a tirade.

"Why aren't you more upset about this?"

"Inside, I'm boiling. But in the past, I've made things worse by responding in the heat of the moment. I'm not sure the best way to handle it— whether to blow up and attack back, or calmly call them out on it, or ignore it. My first choice would be blowing up, so that's probably the wrong one. I'll talk to Irisa and see what she thinks. I really hate the idea of ignoring it."

"Attacks about my designs are one thing; I'm used to critics. But personal ones? Calling me a slut? Suggesting I'm using you? Taking shots at my character when they've never even met me?" She shook her head.

He pulled her into his arms. "I'm sorry, Sunshine. It burns me up to see people saying things about you, but when they're my fans... that makes it so much worse."

Too upset to remain still, she shimmed out of his hold. The flowers lay on the table like drops of sunbeams. "I should take care of these." Moving quickly, she brought them into the kitchen and set about trimming stems and arranging the blooms in her vase.

"Audrey." Luke's hands closed over her shoulders.

"I think these will look nice in the bedroom, don't you? That way, they'll be the first thing I see when I wake up."

"I'd rather be the first thing you see." He turned her to face him and cupped her chin in his hand. "This thing with the fans will blow over."

She swallowed hard and nodded. "Of course it will."

"Come on. It's a nice day. Let's go for a walk. How about the High Line? The guys are still in town. It'll be good to get the whole group together."

She forced a smile because he seemed to need to see it. "I'd like that."

"Good." He picked up the vase and led her by the hand into her bedroom area. After shifting aside a stack of paperback novels, he set the vase on the small table by the window. "If you wake up facing the window, you'll see the flowers. If you wake up facing the door, you'll see me. That's a good compromise."

"What happens if I wake up facing the ceiling?"

"You could always install a mirror up there. I'd like that."

A real smile overtook her fake one. "No."

He shrugged. "No problem. I have a good imagination. Anyway, you'll need sunglasses and some type of hat for today. We're going incognito."

"No trench coat?"

A half-smile quirked at his lips. "We'll save

that one for later."

"Give me a minute to change. It's too hot outside for pants." She peered into her closet, dismissing several options. After the remark about her thighs, wearing shorts wasn't too appealing.

Luke joined her and pulled down a floppy red straw beach hat from the top shelf. "Wear this one."

"Sure." It would disguise most of her face.

Strong hands clasped her waist. "Let me help you." He pulled her tank top over her torso and gently lifted it over her head. When she lowered her arms, he kissed her lips, then moved down to place kisses on each shoulder. Then the hollow of her throat, and he continued kissing his way to the valley between her breasts. He rested his forehead there for a moment, breathing deep while his arms banded around her.

Audrey threaded her fingers in his hair and held him close. He kissed her like he cherished her. Drenched in gratitude and caring and wanting and needing, she tightened her hold.

He knelt before her, kissed a trail to her waistband, and then hooked his thumbs into the clingy fabric. Working the pants down her hips, then down her thighs, he kissed every exposed inch along the way. They pooled at her ankles and he helped her step free, then he glided his hands along her body as he stood. "No question about it, your thighs are perfect."

Heat flushed into her cheeks and pleasure flushed into her soul. "I'm glad you think so."

"Tonight, we can come back here and I can show you over and over again." The light in his eyes, that sexy smile, and the determination in his features, almost made her forget about all of the drama with the fans.

"It's a date." She pulled out a casual navy and white striped t-shirt dress and red flats with thin straps that laced around her ankles. Complementary to Luke's outfit of a white v-neck t-shirt and navy shorts, but not too matched. She needed to feel like they belonged together, especially after so many of the hateful comments suggested otherwise.

CHAPTER TEN

For the first time in his career, he resented the fans. Luke shoved his phone into his pocket and leaned his head against the booth. The hotel pub in Chicago's North Side where he was due to meet the next contestant had great atmosphere, but he couldn't enjoy it. A week had passed since the first negative comments appeared, and they didn't show signs of slowing down. If anything, they'd increased. He was pissed off and baffled by why the fans cared so much about who he spent his time with.

Irisa had advised Audrey and him to not engage or respond, but holding his tongue was killing him.

He sipped his Guinness and stewed.

Beside him, Irisa had her laptop open. She'd accompanied him to Chicago in place of Ivan, claiming that she would be lonely at home with her fiancé away on a long road trip. Luke figured the real reason she'd come along for the ride was more as babysitter than to cover camera duties, in case he snapped under the pressure. She knew him well. "The poll for selecting the new band's name has a clear favorite. Wild Intention is leading by twenty thousand votes."

"Huh." He continued to drink, focused on the

door, thoughts on Audrey and what she was doing. She'd headed to Florida to visit her parents a few days earlier.

"Shit," Irisa exclaimed under her breath, then glanced over at him. "There's a new thread in the fan page forum, dedicated to trashing Audrey."

"Are you fucking kidding me? On our own website?" He yanked the computer away from her and it around to see the screen. "Fucking assholes. No more ignoring this." Pushing back from the bar, he got to his feet and shoved a finger in Irisa's face, his stool scraped the floor as angrily as he felt. "Ignoring it looks like I'm condoning it. And I'm not."

She pulled back her computer and spoke too calmly for Luke's taste. "I'll post something in the forum."

"I can do it." He grabbed at the laptop.

"No." Irisa handily swiped her computer out of his reach. "You're too angry and will go off on a rant. I'll do it."

She was right, of course, but the urge to smash something burned hot in his veins. He took out his frustration on the dart board until the red haze receded.

"Luke," Irisa waved him to the table and turned her screen to face him. "Check it out."

Moderator: Hey guys, this is supposed to be a fun place, not a hateful space. And while The Fury always loves hearing from their fans, we will not tolerate malicious, hateful threads or comments toward anyone—band member or not.

4EverLuke'sGirl: But we're trying to help Luke!

Moderator: Those who continue to post disparaging remarks will have their fan club privileges revoked immediately and permanently.

Luke shook his head. "They're trying to *help* me? What—they think all my brains have headed south?"

"Apparently. I also deleted the thread. This isn't going to stop them from starting their own thread somewhere else, but they won't be able to do it on our own site anymore."

"What about my personal pages? I delete comments as I see them, but keeping up with it is a full time job."

"Jayne and I will help with your stuff. We divvied up all the band's sites and pages and are monitoring those."

"I appreciate it." His phone vibrated again, followed by the distinctive ring of his video chat. Happiness streaked through the annoyance. "That'll be Audrey."

He engaged the chat and her image came to life on the screen. Her hair, pulled back in a high ponytail, put all the focus on her face. Her features looked a little pale. Odd, considering she was in a beach town and supposed to be soaking up the sun. Her expressive eyes were missing their spark.

"Hey, Sunshine. How's the visit going?"

"It's nice seeing my folks. How did your fan audition go?"

"It didn't start yet. Oh, and Irisa's here." He tilted the phone enough for Irisa to wave at the screen. "You look upset."

"I... Your fans are getting worse. They aren't

just leaving comments on your page or the band's page, now they're clogging up my social media accounts with the comments, too. Pictures I posted of items from my collection and from the runway show now have comments like, *Better thank Luke for this success, bitch* and *He'll see through you eventually* and *Hey user, leave Luke alone.* I don't have control over comments on certain sites. My only option would be to shut down my page or profile, but I can't do that. I need to be reachable. I can't risk losing business, but if a potential client sees these messages, it might push them away from me. This is almost like slander."

There had to be something he could do. This was out of control. "I'm hiring an attorney and the best egghead money can buy. No one's going to fuck with you or your business."

"I'm on it." Irisa made a sound of disgust and immediately began typing on her laptop.

Luke moved the phone closer to his face. Reaching through and touching her would be the only thing to make him feel better. "I wish I was there with you."

"Me too."

"I can fly down to see you tomorrow."

"No. Don't change your plans. I'm all right." The quaver in her voice didn't sit well with him. "I just needed to vent for a minute."

"I'll get to hold you in a few days." The reminder was for her, but also for himself. The only thing getting him through was her planned visit to L.A. and Vegas with him.

Lines formed on her forehead and she bit her

lip. He could see her hands wring together. "I'm not sure my coming out to visit is a good idea, given the circumstances. You don't need me to be physically there for the launch party. You guys already have the clothes you want."

"No." He shot to his feet, upsetting the water glasses he'd ignored earlier. "No fucking way. They aren't taking this away from us. You have your flight already set. We'll wear goddamn wigs, hats, and sunglasses the whole time if you want, but I need to see you. And I need you at that party."

"We can talk about it later." She turned and her focus moved off camera for a moment. "My mom wants to go out for drinks. I have to go."

"I'll call you back tonight." He ended the call and tossed the phone on the table before dropping back into his seat. "I don't fucking understand this. I get that the fans feel like they know me pretty well, but the reality is that they don't. I've given everything to them, and this is what happens? Not that I'd wish this on Zander and Jayne, but no one seems to be freaking out about them being together."

Irisa sighed and sipped her wine. "While the group as a whole has fans, you each have your own core base too. I guess yours are just more protective, vocal, or jealous. Maybe a combination of all three. I'm not blaming you for being fan-friendly, but you've always been very accessible, and some girls think they actually have a shot with you. Look at what happened with Mikala. I think jealousy is a huge factor here."

"Along with being judgmental. And

misinformed. They've had the wrong idea about her from the beginning. I need to set it straight."

"Luke—"

"No. I waited like you wanted and it hasn't done any good. I'm not going to sit back any longer while my woman gets trashed."

"I understand where you're coming from, but you need to be calm when you post. And to be perfectly honest, whatever you write may not change their opinions anyway. You know you can't reason with crazy."

The contestant, Steve, entered the pub holding hands with a woman. Luke stifled a sigh. Exhausted and stressed didn't make well for a good night, but he pasted on a smile to greet them.

"Hey, man." He shook hands. "Good to meet you."

"Thanks. This is my girlfriend Ursula. It's cool if she watches, right?"

"Sure." He waited until they'd met Irisa, then said, "Let's head to the conference room and get started. You're performing *My Fist, Your Face*, right?"

"Right."

Steve was the opposite of Hugh— overconfident. He sang well but something about him seemed a little too smug, a little too much like Owen. Luke didn't want his dislike of Owen to color his initial impression of Steve, so after the audition, he invited Steve and Ursula back to the pub for drinks and conversation.

All Steve wanted to do was drink beer and talk about concerts and music. That suited Luke fine and he warmed up more to the contest hopeful. Ursula was quiet for the first half of the night, chatting with them off and on, but the more she drank, the more she talked, and then sang and danced by the table. By the end of the night, she'd dragged first Luke, then Irisa to the bar to sing karaoke with her. The tune she'd selected was the one Luke had sang to Audrey while on Jett's show.

He took it as a sign. And when he bade them goodnight, he sat down at the bar with Irisa's computer and drafted out his message to his fans.

Guys, lately you may have seen me photographed with a sexy brunette. I'd like to introduce you all to Audrey. She's an amazing woman who is kind, talented, and has a huge heart. I've never been this happy and I hope you'll all celebrate my happiness with me. On a related note, there have been a lot of rumors flying around that don't hold any truth. While I can appreciate concerns, I'm the best judge of who and what is best for me. Please respect my wishes to keep all posted comments on this page positive. Thank you, Luke

He hit *Post*. Hopefully, it would be enough to end the drama.

CHAPTER ELEVEN

Halfway between Tampa and Los Angeles, Audrey was convinced she'd made the wrong decision in visiting Luke. She wanted to see him, and he'd said he'd needed her, but the recent backlash from his fans in response to his statement about their relationship was enough to make her want to hide in her apartment.

He'd asked them to refrain from posting mean comments on his pages. They'd respected his wishes, but redoubled their efforts by peppering her pages instead.

Baseball cap tugged low, she dug through her bag and unearthed a bottle of water and a chocolate bar. Seeing insults daily cut through her self-confidence. *Fat, ugly, troll, slut, user, bitch, whore...* the list went on and on. Renee, her fierce warrior of an assistant, had insisted on taking over most of the posting. She'd temporarily shut down two of the pages that had spiraled out of control.

A lengthy conversation with the lawyer Luke had hired had lead her to believe there wasn't much that could be done from a legal standpoint. Common sense dictated the comments would eventually stop. Audrey would just be in hell until that happened.

As the plane circled and then touched down at LAX, excitement over seeing him outweighed everything else. Deplaning took too long and she grew impatient. Finally released, she rushed as fast as she could to baggage claim. She didn't bother looking for her luggage snaking around on the baggage tram. Instead she scanned every face, expecting to see Luke.

At long last she recognized his swagger cutting an impressive swath through the crowd. He met her gaze and a huge grin spread across his face. "Hey, Sunshine," he hollered. And then she was in his arms, breathing him in and holding him close.

"Goddamn, it's good to see you." His lips descended and captured hers. She wasn't prepared for the emotion welling in her soul.

Ten days had passed since she'd kissed him goodbye at the airport in New York. Ten days wasn't long enough to miss someone the way she missed him. Neither of them were returning from war or a long journey. But it didn't matter. The last week and a half sure had felt like a constant barrage of attacks. Perhaps that was it. Pressing in tighter, she deepened the kiss.

The flash of a camera light too close to her face startled her. Audrey pulled back, but Luke tucked her against his chest and glared at the camera's owner. He smiled again when he glanced down at her. "Let's grab your bags. My driver's waiting for us outside. It's about a twenty minute drive to my place."

He pointed out some landmarks during the drive, and kept touching her—on her leg, her arm, her face, her hair.

She leaned against him, fully relaxing for the first time in days.

"My place is right up here." He pointed to a three story modern-design home on their right. The car pulled in to a long and gated driveway.

"You live on the beach?" He'd told her he lived in Hermosa Beach, but she hadn't realized his house was beach-front property. The sand colored house blended in with seaside colors. Four palm trees lined one side of the property, and a privacy fence the color of driftwood surrounded the home. Three stories, two balconies, and a large patio for the bottom level.

He bade the driver goodbye and carried her luggage into the house. "I'll give you the tour."

She slipped her hand in his and followed him.

"Living room." Sparsely decorated with pale gray furniture and a fireplace in the corner, the room had a light and airy feel, thanks to white walls and sandy wood floors, a set of sliding glass doors to the second-level balcony, and two bay windows letting in tons of natural light. She could picture Luke stretched out on the couch after a long day. Or them together on the balcony, sharing a drink after dinner.

"Kitchen." Dark wood cabinets, sleek appliances, with counter tops and tiles the color of polished sea shells, the open-concept room overlooked the dining and living room. He showed her his collection of beer mugs—souvenirs from his travels around the world. An image struck her, of cooking with Luke, lingering over touches and tastes of each other. Or putting that breakfast bar to better use... it was the perfect height for a more intimate form of cooking, if the bedroom was too far away.

"Down the hall is an extra guest bedroom and bathroom. It's boring. Let's head upstairs."

"Is that where the magic happens?" She followed him up a spiral staircase with an overhead skylight to the top level of the home.

"I guess we'll find out tonight." He paused in the hall, winked at her, and then pointed to his left. "My bedroom." The master suite faced the ocean and had its own balcony. Dark furniture polished to a high shine set off pale gray walls. A large TV hung on the wall opposite the bed, next to a shelf containing a stack of action movies and a collection of true crime novels.

She glanced at the bed, twice the size of hers, with its custom headboard covered in what she knew to be a very pricey fabric. Being in that bed with him later... a shiver of anticipation ran through her.

The amazing view of the ocean drew her onto the balcony, decorated with two lounge chairs and a small table. "I would sit out here every day if I had this view."

He caged her in against the railing, arms bracketing her on both sides. "I would sit out here and think about you. I never thought I'd actually have you here, in my space."

"I like being able to picture you here. I'm glad I got to see it. Now I'll know what to imagine when you're back here and I'm in New York."

The light in his eyes dimmed. "Let's finish up the tour."

The sea theme continued through the master bath, with pale shades, and light wood and slate gray accents. With two sinks, a jetted tub big enough for two, a separate shower stall, and a large, frosted window for privacy, the room was four times the size of her studio's bathroom.

"Can we use the tub later?"

"We? Hell, you're reading my mind." He linked their hands again. "Anything you want."

He pointed out another bedroom and full bath, then took her down to the lowest level. "Here we have space that I'm not using."

A powder room, a dry-bar, a large room with sliding glass doors that led onto a patio and faced the ocean, and a separate room that could be another bedroom or office. The entire floor was bigger than her *Audrey Pierce Designs* space.

"This is incredible. Really, I love the entire house."

"I'm glad you like it. I'd hoped you would. I want you to feel at home." He looked like he wanted to say something more, but then he pulled out his phone and mildly swore. "I have my last fan audition at three o'clock. Come with me? I need a camera person."

"Who is it with?"

"Nicole DiGiovanni, a twenty-two year old woman from Anaheim. She told Jayne that she would be bringing a small group of women with her as support."

Her heart plummeted. She shook her head, held

up her hands, and backed up a step. "No thanks. I don't want to be subjected to any more mean comments."

He frowned and moved toward her. "I'm not going to let anyone say anything mean about you or to you."

"I'm sure they'll take pictures and they'll want to post those pictures..." And then the comments would appear... cutting her to pieces. She held a hand to the ache in her stomach.

Luke's expression softened to concern and something else she couldn't name. He cupped his large hands around her face. "Let them see that you're this amazing person who could be their best friend. Who knows, maybe some good comments will start and counteract the bad."

She didn't hold much hope for that, but didn't want to let him down. And he *would* be there with her. "Where are you meeting them?"

"A hotel in Long Beach. She'll do her audition, and then we can grab dinner with her afterward."

She was starved for time with him, and if he really did need her to help with recording, she wanted to be there for him. "I'll go. You'll be there the whole time, right?"

A smile lit his features and then his lips touched hers in a quick kiss. "Absolutely. We need to leave now. Its takes between thirty to forty minutes to get to Long Beach, and I don't want to be late."

"Is your driver coming back or did you call a cab?"

"Actually..." He walked over to a bowl by the

door and picked up a spare set of keys. "Do you want to drive? I can't get behind the wheel for another few months, but as long as you're here, you can use my car. Having you drive it will be better than letting it sit or having someone else along when we'd rather be alone together."

She'd read about him losing his license after the arrest a few months ago. "Can I ask what happened that night?"

"The arrest? The night I found out about you and Dante, I was out on my boat, thinking, and ended up drinking too much. Stupid, reckless mistake. One I take seriously." So solemn and contrite, he held her gaze. She didn't judge him for his mistake, especially not when he'd been hurting then and was so obviously sorry it had happened.

They'd both made mistakes. She'd pulled him in close and hugged him tight. His arms came around her and he rested his head on top of hers. They stayed wrapped together, just holding each other, for a long moment.

An hour later, Audrey stood in the hotel lobby before five sisters ranging in age from eighteen to twenty-six. Nicole, Coco, Serena, Desiree, and Olivia were stereotypically friendly Italians, hugging Luke and her like they were old friends or family.

The youngest sister, Olivia's, brows rose. "Oh, you're *that* woman."

A long, uncomfortable pause followed while Audrey bristled up to defend herself. Luke's hand at the small of her back gave an extra layer of support.

Nicole slapped her sister's shoulder and Olivia

yelped and jumped away. "What my baby sister means is hello and we're happy you're joining us."

With the exception of the baby sister, busy rubbing her arm and mouthing *ow*, the other sisters all smiled at her and echoed the welcome.

After weeks of meanness, the friendly tone was an unexpected surprise. Audrey clung to it. "Thank you. Luke played your demo for me. You have a beautiful voice."

Luke slid his arm around her and lightly squeezed her shoulder. "Let's get started."

Audrey settled into a seat next to Luke in the conference room and set the camera to recording. "We're rolling."

He smiled at her and then into the camera. "Hey, Fury fans, Luke here. I have our final contestant, Nicole. Tell us about how you got started singing."

"I've been singing for as long as I can remember. When I was growing up, my sisters and I would perform musicals in our yard."

"Really? I love that." Audrey smiled at the sisters, and then laughed as all five began talking at once about the musicals, and then again when they broke into song at Luke's request. Finally, they quieted enough for Nicole to audition. She performed *Cut Down*, ending with a standing ovation from her sisters.

The group moved into the hotel restaurant. Over the next hour, the constant chatter and laughter from the sisters helped soothe Audrey's soul. Each one included her in conversation and treated her like family. Being an only child, Audrey didn't fully understand the sibling dynamic, but the women teased and laughed and seemed genuinely delighted by each other's company.

When Luke accompanied two of the sisters to the bar, Olivia moved in to the open seat next to Audrey like she'd been waiting for the chance to talk to her alone.

Unease curled in her stomach. Luke, Nicole, and Serena were at the other end of the room, and Coco and Desiree peered out the windows looking at the bay. All were out of earshot. Olivia had been the quietest with her all afternoon. Audrey raised her brows and smiled. "This is pretty cool, isn't it? I never get tired of looking at the ocean."

Olivia bit her lip, looking pained. "I wanted to apologize for earlier. I was surprised to see you, that's all. I didn't mean anything by it."

"That's all right."

"Nicole says I speak before I think sometimes." She glanced at her sister. "Anyway, you seem really nice. I don't know why the girls online are being so mean. I really hope it stops soon."

The unease fluttered away and for the first time she was happy around Luke's fans. "Thank you. I appreciate that. It's been a really hard time for me."

"I was bullied really badly all through high school, so I know what it's like." The brief sadness darkening Olivia's face tugged at Audrey's heart.

Audrey pulled her in for a hug. "I'm sorry about that. No one should have to go through it."

"The Fury's music really helped me. I was so excited when Nicole won the fan audition because I wanted a chance to say thank you to Luke."

"Definitely tell him. You'll make his day. It's nice Nicole wanted you all here. I'm really glad I got to meet all of you. I'm an only child. I always wanted sisters."

"Try being the youngest. It's like having five moms." She rolled her eyes, but then smiled. "Really, they're the best. They pulled me out when I spiraled too far into a dark place."

"Are things better for you now?" Audrey hated the thought of the sweet girl being under attack.

"Well, I graduated in June, so I don't have to see the people who were mean to me on a daily basis anymore. There's an anti-bullying program in Anaheim that helped me too. I just started volunteering there this month. I want to help people like me."

"I would love to be involved with something like that." She hadn't endured bullying on a daily basis for four years like Olivia, but the weeks of daily attacks were brutal enough for her to understand why some victims made heartbreaking choices. Olivia had sparked an idea. Audrey wanted to take a stand. Fight back. Make a difference. "Can you give me the organization's name?"

"Of course. The program serves all of Southern California. I'll send you a link with their info when I get home." Olivia smiled and then stood. "Come on. Let's join the others."

Audrey walked up to the group arm-in-arm with Olivia. Apparently one-on-one was the way to convince people she wasn't a horrible human being.

Five people down... five million to go.

CHAPTER TWELVE

The Las Vegas night club looked like someone had poured all of the lights and glitter found on The Strip into a single room. Streamers and balloons, appetizers and alcohol, friends and colleagues and well-wishers, all shiny and sparkly and over the top, and all in support of The Fury and their newest venture. A floor to ceiling image of the Furious Records logo lit up one wall. Every time Luke saw it, pride and excitement shot through him.

He'd worked his ass off getting the evening to come together. Every band member had played a part. And Audrey had helped tie it all together. In her gold dress, threaded with a hint of shimmer, she sparkled even more than usual—and he wasn't the only one who noticed. Heads turned, people stared, and more than one man found an excuse to talk to her.

She smiled up at him. The past two days with her had been magic. Ever since the afternoon with the warm, welcoming sisters, she'd been happier. Staying offline had helped, too. When he hadn't been with the band, he'd kept her as occupied as possible, on the beach and in the bedroom, exhausting them both so much the idea of turning on a computer or checking email seemed too taxing.

He'd been pleasantly surprised when she brought up the idea of working with an anti-bullying program. His girl was fighter in her own way and he'd support her in anything.

Zander tapped his shoulder. "It's time."

Luke released Audrey's hand and followed his best friend to the small stage. He couldn't wait to announce the contest winners. The decision had been tough. He'd gone back and forth between Hugh and Nicole. The other guys hadn't had easy times deciding either. In the end, he'd gone with his gut.

People gathered around them. The contestants stood close by while Zander gave a speech about being grateful for opportunities and how the band had enjoyed every audition. Luke raised his brow at that. Not *every* audition. Every contestant except Mikala was in attendance.

"We'd like everyone to meet the members of Wild Intention. Lead singer, Hugh Tremont. Drummer, Chelsea Jankowski. Bass guitar, Autumn Grainger. And lead guitar, Spike Peters. Congratulations, guys. We're excited to work with you."

As applause and cheers rang out, Luke made his way over to Hugh. "Congrats, bud."

Blond hair flopping over his forehead, Hugh hugged him hard. "Thank you. I promise I won't let you down."

Nicole was next in line, congratulating Hugh. Then she smiled at Luke and held out her hand. "Thank you for the opportunity."

He leaned in until others were out of earshot. "I

have something else in mind for you. I like the dynamic you share with your sisters. Give me a few weeks to get things going with this band and then give me a call. I'd like to see if we can do something with all five of you."

Her eyes widened. "They're going to flip out. So cool. Thank you." After hugging him, she almost tackled Audrey with another hug, and then left to call her sisters.

Shaking his head at the amount of confetti falling from the ceiling, and ridiculously pleased and relieved that the party had gone off without a hitch, Luke turned to Audrey. "Want to dance?"

She placed her hand in his. "Love to."

He led her onto the crowded floor. Zander and Jayne danced close by. He waved and then pulled Audrey into his arms. They fit together well, her head on his shoulder, his hands on her back. She fit so much of his life. He could already imagine her sharing his space.

Her fingers brushed the back of his neck and she sighed. "This is nice."

"This is perfect. All the work's done now. We can relax for the rest of the night." His hand spanned her low back. He nudged her closer to him. He figured another hour would be enough for putting in an appearance. Then he could get Audrey back to their hotel suite and have her all to himself.

The song ended and they headed in search of champagne. Brendan, Landry, and Irisa stood near a large twisted metal sculpture. Holding Audrey's hand, he detoured in that direction. Zander and Jayne joined a moment later. Luke chatted, one eye and one ear on the conversation and the other on how Audrey was fitting into the group. Irisa and Jayne and Audrey were already a tight trio. No problems there. Brendan liked everyone and teased her like a kid sister, and she'd even gotten Landry, the least talkative and most stoic, to smile. Zander's opinion mattered, and his oldest friend kept grinning at him and gave him a thumbs up.

"Excuse me, guys." Donnie Snell, a reporter for one of the music industry's widest-read rag magazines, approached the group with phone in hand. "I'm doing a story on the party. Can I get a few words?"

"Sure." Zander waved him in, grimacing over Donnie's head, and shifted Jayne to his other side. Luke didn't blame him. Something about Donnie made him want to wash his hands after they spoke. He didn't want the guy near Audrey either. Donnie's column always stank of sensationalized stories. Not inviting him to the party hadn't stopped him. He'd arrived as another reporter's guest.

"First, congratulations on your new label." He started recording using his phone. "Do you have anything to say to Excite Records for releasing you?"

Brendan leaned over and spoke into the phone. "We're excited about the opportunities we have coming up with Furious Records, and especially working with Wild Intention."

Luke patted him on the back and echoed what he said.

Donnie turned to him. "You seem to be recovered from your fashion show brawl with Owen

Riess. Can you give our readers a sense of what you were thinking that night?"

To his right, Audrey stiffened. Luke linked hands with her and rubbed his thumb over her knuckles. "That night, I was thinking about how talented the designer is. Everyone should check out Audrey Pierce's collection."

"*That's* what you were thinking?" Donnie shook his head and then thrust his phone in Audrey's direction. "How about you? How did it feel to have a fight break out at your show?"

Audrey offered him a calm expression and an apologetic smile. "We're here to celebrate Furious Records and Wild Intention. I'd rather keep the attention on them."

"All right, little lady, we can do that. Much like The Fury is launching the careers of Wild Intention's members, Excite's president, Vance Dubrow was responsible for launching the careers of Rob Hawke and Luke Thompson, both of whom you're intimately acquainted with. How does it feel to be accused by Luke's fans of using him to promote your brand?"

What the fuck? Luke pushed forward and growled, "Now hold up there..."

Donnie side-stepped him and shoved the phone closer to Audrey. "And a follow-up: What about their accusations of your recently-ended relationship with Rob, whom they believe you used to break into the music world? Tell me, are the fans correct in their assumptions or are they operating from a basis of jealousy?"

Pulse pounding, heat spreading through

stiffened muscles, Luke grabbed hold of the phone and glowered at Donnie. He turned off the recording and paged through the app, looking to delete the conversation. "You're part of the problem, trying to stir up shit for readers and fans to latch onto, and spew out even more crap. People like you are encouraging hate with loaded questions like that, which can snowball into bullying, all for the sake of a few clicks on your website so you can sell more ads."

Donnie's lips set in a thin line. He pulled the phone away. "That's an interesting way to avoid answering the question, Luke. Perhaps Ms. Pierce would like to answer the question on her own? Maybe you're worried about what she'll say?"

He shifted to block Audrey from Donnie's view. "She doesn't have to talk to you."

But Audrey's hand met his forearm and she squeezed and then stepped forward. "The comments are hurtful because they aren't true. I can stand here and say I'm not a user or opportunistic, or any of the other terms they've called me, but my doing so isn't going to change peoples' opinions. Everyone has a right to believe what they want to believe but the sad part is they're forming their opinion based on misinformation, speculation, or fabrication."

Luke wrapped his arm around her and stared Donnie down, daring him to ask another question. Audrey was smart, a fast-thinker, and eloquent.

Donnie spun from one end of their half-circle to the other as the band closed ranks around their newest addition.

Zander cleared his throat, drawing the reporter's

attention. "Thanks for chatting with us. We'll overlook that you crashed our party and let you move on to other guests now."

Donnie looked over Audrey's shoulder and his eyes lit up. "There's the next guy I was looking for. Owen Riess, how are you?"

Fuck. Temper flashed from annoyance to seething in the space of a heartbeat. Luke turned and came face-to-face with Owen. He definitely hadn't been on the guest list. "What the hell are you doing here?"

"Couldn't resist stopping by to see this little party. The guy at the door let us in." The singer had his band mates from Swindle Ox and his girlfriend with him. They closed in around Owen, mirroring the way The Fury surrounded Luke.

Tension charged the air as the groups stared at each other.

"This is ridiculous," Landry mumbled on Luke's left. "We look like two musically-inclined rival gangs getting ready to rumble."

"I know," Brendan, on his right, added. "I feel the urge to start snapping my fingers and breaking into song."

At the image, Luke huffed out a laugh. And Owen's gaze narrowed further.

Donnie pushed his way into the middle of the pack, phone in hand. "This is the first time you've seen each other since the fashion show?"

"You mean, since Luke attacked me." Owen crossed his arms over his chest, the light of battle in his eyes.

Rehashing the events of that night was getting

old. "I didn't throw the first punch. But I don't back down from a fight." He wouldn't get into one now. Audrey's hands, resting on his back, were a gentle reminder to keep a level head.

Owen cracked his knuckles and lumbered too close into Luke's space. "Is that an invitation to go again?"

Luke drew himself up to full height and tensed his muscles out of habit, but he didn't back down. He outweighed Owen by a solid thirty pounds and had him beat a good four inches in height. Brendan and Landry closed ranks, moving just a bit in front of him. He didn't need his friends to fight his battles, but none of them wanted to end up in the headlines again for the wrong reason. Two bar fights on their last tour were good reasons to hold back. "I'm not fighting you here. First of all, you weren't invited. So unless you want security to escort you out, I suggest you leave."

Owen's gaze tracked to Audrey, and then her hold on Luke's jacket. "You're letting your girlfriend call the shots? Is that it? You really are a pussy."

Audrey's hands tightened. Luke reached one arm behind him and held her hip, silently communicating he'd keep his cool. "I'd rather make my girlfriend happy than waste the night fighting with you. As someone wise once reminded me, we're not two kids fighting on a playground. So yeah, if she asks me not to fight, I'm not going to fight."

Vanessa moved next to Owen. She didn't look happy about Owen's behavior at all. "Baby, he's right. Come on. You're causing a scene."

Glaring at him, Owen growled, "This isn't over." He allowed Vanessa to draw him away. Swindle Ox followed. And Donnie disappeared.

Luke let out a breath. He wrapped his arm around Audrey's waist and faced his band. "Thanks for standing with me. You all helped me keep my cool."

"We would've had your back either way." Landry rolled his shoulders and cracked his neck. "Bar?"

"Sure."

The group moved as a unit. Audrey paused by an empty, narrow alcove and pulled Luke inside.

"What's up?"

She slid her arms up his chest and around his neck. "Thank you for not fighting."

He clamped his hands on her hips. The soft material of her dress bunched under his flexing fingers. "Anything for you, Sunshine."

"Kiss me?" Five-inch heels brought the top of her head level with his chin. She tilted her face up and her fingers glided into his hair to pull his mouth down to meet hers.

With a groan, he angled his head and deepened the kiss. Her tongue played and stroked against his and he couldn't get enough. Laughter and conversations interrupted the moment and reminded him they weren't in their room, they were in a temporarily empty spot in a very crowded party.

He lifted his head. "How about that champagne?"

"Please."

"You wait here. I'll grab it, and then we can sneak off to our room."

"I like your thinking."

He kissed Audrey's temple and adjusted his clothes and then headed out.

**

Audrey stood tucked away in the private alcove, waiting for Luke. Footsteps drew closer, too soon for Luke to have reached the bar and returned.

"Audrey." Rob Hawke walked toward her with a warm smile. Although their relationship had been trying, their breakup had been amicable. He leaned in to brush a kiss on her cheek. "Good to see you."

"How are you?" She hadn't seen him since a few months earlier when he'd stopped in the studio to pick up the clothes he'd ordered. The faint lines around his eyes had deepened some and more flecks of gray dotted his brown hair.

"Good, good. Where's Luke?"

"Getting drinks at the bar. Are you here alone?"

"My date's on a smoke break. I saw the alcove and thought I could hide from the craziness until she comes back." He leaned in and lowered his voice. "Are you holding up okay?"

"Sure. The party's fun."

"Not what I meant. I heard Luke going off at Donnie and the questions he asked you. I didn't realize you were having bullying issues."

She sighed and twisted the chain strap of her clutch purse around her fingers. "It started a few weeks ago. They're pretty vicious."

"I'm sorry, sweetie." His hand rested on her shoulder for the briefest moment. "That situation isn't fun, but the comments and attention will die down eventually."

She gripped her clutch tighter. "So, if you heard the questions he asked, you know the gist of how the mean comments started."

"We know our relationship wasn't based on using each other, and I know you well enough to be sure that your relationship with Luke isn't either. Other people's opinions don't concern me. I do the best I can. I let my work speak for itself. I don't owe anyone an explanation for the way I live my life."

"But the court of public opinion can hurt your livelihood. I think it's affecting mine."

He shrugged. "You're smart and talented. Whatever happens, you adjust to it. Just live your life and be happy."

"You always did give good advice."

"The benefits of age." He winked at her.

"Rob, here you are." Donnie Snell's voice rang out. "And with Audrey too. Looks like I interrupted a cozy conversation."

Her back stiffened. She didn't like this guy one bit. "I'll let you guys chat."

"No need to leave, Ms. Pierce."

"Actually, there is."

Rob waved goodbye. "Aud, send me that jacket Luke wore in the fashion show. I want it for my Fall tour."

If Donnie hadn't been standing there, she would have hugged Rob. "I will. Thanks."

Rob's advice echoing in her head, she left the

alcove in search of Luke.

He met her halfway into her trek across the crowded room. Two glasses in hand and a bottle of bubbly all to themselves. "Ready to go?"

"Yes. Donnie came into the alcove while I was talking to Rob. Something about that guy puts my back up. Donnie, I mean, not Rob."

He stopped walking. "Rob's here? I heard someone mention him but I haven't seen him."

She nodded. "He came in to wait while his date was on a smoke break."

"Huh."

"What's that mean?"

"Nothing."

Not nothing. She stepped in front of him. "What is it?"

"Did he say anything?"

"Well, we didn't communicate via mime."

"Cute."

She smiled. "He actually gave me some good advice about living my life and not worrying so much about other people's opinion. It's still going to be hard when they're calling me all those awful names, or trashing my looks, but I'll really try not to let it get me down."

"If I didn't have both hands full, I'd lift you up right now and spin you around to celebrate. Let's get to the room so I can show you how happy that makes me."

The room had a spectacular view of The Strip. Luke set down the glasses and poured the champagne. He gave her a glass then held his up in toast. "To you, for being my saving grace. And for not worrying about the jealous words of other girls."

Audrey grinned. "And to you, for holding your temper with Owen. I'm really proud of you." Bubbles tickled her tongue. She set the glass aside and walked toward him, pausing for a moment to switch off the light. Darkness bathed the room, except for the lights coming in from the window.

She caressed her way up his shirt, over his hard pecs then reached up and loosened his tie. One-handed, he yanked at the knot and tore the silken strip from around his neck, then his jacket followed to the floor.

His familiar strong hands stroked from her shoulders to her waist, repeating the caress up and down, and up and down. Her head fell back when he cupped her breasts, and clever fingers stroked and pinched until she moaned.

Hands unsteady, she pulled at the buttons lining the front of his shirt, popping off two in her hurry to touch his skin.

"Sunshine." He kissed her shoulder, on the edge of where the dress met bare skin, and then pulled the fabric down, trapping her arms against her sides. Lips and tongue traced along her skin. He pulled lower, grabbing both dress and bra and pulling them to her waist.

With her hands trapped, she could only feel as he layered sensation on sensation. Strong fingers kneaded into her back. He closed his mouth over the peak of one breast and gave the other attention with his hand, molding, tweaking, and tugging a direct path to her core. Her hands fisted at her sides and she swayed toward him.

Luke smiled and tugged the dress to the floor. He picked her up and laid her on the bed. She reached for him, but her hands met his hair as he licked a path down her stomach, and then lower. His mouth played and his fingers glided inside, knowledgeable in their aim.

Clutching his hair, she came apart, clamping her legs around his shoulders to keep him close.

"Don't worry, Sunshine, I'm not going anywhere far." He inched his way up her body, then stood and shucked off his pants and boxers.

When he joined her on the bed, she rolled them over until she straddled him. "My turn."

The scrape of her nails down his torso resulted in an intake of breath and muscles drawing tight. Teases of her fingertips along his arms and legs caused him to shift and moan. Kisses placed anywhere made him sigh. She worked her way down his stomach and sat between his legs. His erection jutted before her. She wrapped her hands around him, and stroked in the firm grasp he preferred. She loved the hiss he'd make when she twisted her hand at the top of her stroke, and the way his hips jerked off the bed when she closed her mouth over him and swallowed him down.

His hands tangled in her hair, fisted, tightened, and his movements grew restless. He pulled her off of him, rolled her over, and thrust inside.

"Audrey." Her name trembled out mixed with a groan. He linked their hands together by her head and nipped at her lips.

She wrapped her legs around his waist, increasing the pace of his snapping hips, and felt his racing heart beat in time with hers.

Faster and faster, she chased pleasure until Luke's body tightened and he ground his pelvis into hers. The pressure triggered and extended her release and as she came around him, he thrust hard twice more and then grunted his own.

She drifted her hands along his damp back as his breathing slowed.

"I'll move as soon as I have energy, I promise." He kissed her temple and then heaved himself off of her. He rolled onto his back and took her with him.

Audrey snuggled into his side, sleepy and sated. If only it could always be this way... "I'm not ready to go back to New York yet."

"You like it out here?" His hand stroked along her side.

She stretched and sighed. "I love being in your beach house. It'll be hard going back to my tiny little box of an apartment."

"Would you ever consider moving? You could just as easily work from here as you can in New York."

Was he asking her to move in with him? Was she ready for that? "I haven't thought that far ahead. My leases for both the apartment and the design studio are coming up for renewal soon. Once I receive the paperwork, if I'm not renewing, I'll have thirty days to tell them."

"So I have two weeks to convince you Cali is best before we return to New York. Mission accepted."

She grinned. It definitely sounded like he wanted her close by. "You don't have to come back with me if you'd rather stay in Cali."

"I'd rather stay with you, wherever that is. You're not getting rid of me that easily."

"I don't want to. In case you haven't noticed, I like having you around." Even though they'd slept together almost every night while in New York, he'd still kept the hotel room. But things had changed between them and she didn't see the need for it any longer. Did he? She took a deep breath and lowered her focus to the sheets. "When we get back, you don't need to get a hotel room. Unless you want it. And it's fine if you want it. I just thought that since we've been—"

He raised up on one elbow and pinched her chin gingerly between his index finger and thumb. Her breath caught at his serious, intense, blazing blue stare. "You're letting me stay with you?"

"I'll give you a key, too. That way you're not stuck inside or locked out if I'm not home."

"Sounds like a good deal to me." A grin spread across his features, as bright as the lights of The Strip. He wrapped his arms around her and his hand resumed the slow stroke along her side.

She settled against him in the cocoon of soft sheets. No one except Renee had a key to her apartment. And that was just for emergencies like locking herself out. She'd never given Dante a key. Or Rob. But she'd offered one to Luke without hesitation.

Maybe it was just a key to her apartment.

But maybe it was more.

***

After a night of bliss, Luke sang while he packed his things for the return trip to L.A. Audrey had joined Jayne for breakfast in Zander and Jayne's suite.

His phone lit up with Irisa's number. "Hey."

"Donnie's article was just released. It's not good. He shared it on your page, too. I wanted you to see it before I deleted it. Renee must have removed it from Audrey's page because it's not there."

"That bad, huh?" Frowning, he opened his laptop.

"I'm handling it, so don't overreact. Call me when you and Audrey have seen it."

He tossed his phone aside. Donnie Snell's article on their launch party had made his magazine's front page news story. One photo showed Luke standing head to head with Owen. They looked like they were about to come to blows. Headline: *Ready to Rumble.* The article went on to list choice sound bites that painted both men as blood-thirsty fighters. Not great, but not awful. Plus, anyone in attendance at the party could attest that no fight had broken out.

Another photo showed Audrey and Rob standing close together in the alcove. Rob's lips were on her cheek. Headline: *Secret Rendezvous?* The article talked about a clandestine moment for the couple while their significant others were otherwise occupied. The picture alone was enough to send fire through his blood. The hint of Audrey cheating on him and planning on leaving him for

Rob sent the savage beast deep within beating his wings against his cage. But he knew Audrey would never hurt him like that.

Audrey sauntered into the room. She glanced at his face and hers immediately creased in concern. "What's wrong?"

That emotion couldn't be faked, right? Her invitation to basically live with her in New York had actually happened, right? *Calm the fuck down, Thompson.* Reminding himself that Donnie always twisted words and situations, and that he again knew Audrey would never betray him, he motioned her over. "There's something you need to see."

She dropped down beside him on the bed, reading the article over his shoulder. Little hisses and squeaks sounded, and then she shifted and gripped his forearm hard, her eyes wide and earnest. "I swear nothing happened. He gave me a quick peck hello on the cheek. More of an air kiss, really. That's it. I had no idea he was even at the party until I saw him. I don't want him back and he doesn't want me. I only want you."

Her words quieted his heart. Luke lifted his arm until she'd detached her grip, and then wrapped it around her waist. He dropped a kiss on her bare shoulder. "I trust you. Donnie does this kind of thing all the time."

"Then why did you guys agree to talk to him at all?"

"Saying no only makes things worse. He was probably ticked off that I called him out on what he was doing. This is his way of retaliating. He got me too." He pulled up the article with Owen and him.

"See?"

"He rearranged things that were said. You held yourself in control the whole time. He's making up seventy-five percent of this story."

He nodded. "Irisa is already on it. I'm sure she sent it to our legal team, just in case. Not everyone realizes Donnie's true M.O., so when the fans read the article, they might not react well."

"Might not react well is an understatement." Audrey lifted her gaze from the screen. "I'm not sure if I want to see the comments."

He didn't want anything to further dull the sparkle in her eyes. "I'll look. Why don't you make sure you have everything packed?"

She kissed him then, long and deep, and wrapped herself around him. When his head was completely mixed up, she pulled away. "Thank you."

He scrolled to the comments when she left the room.

They weren't good. Harsh and unnecessary were more like it, and the ones on his page were even worse.

Fury_Fan_4ever: BUSTED! Ha Ha! Good luck explaining this one to him, whore. Who else are you going to scam into helping you next?

01_Fury_Fan: She's cheating on Luke. Rob's cheating on his girl. Both of them deserve each other. Ew.

Mikala_Mason: See??? She is a USER! Luke will be crushed. I hope that SLUT falls over and DIES! BITCH!

The forcefulness of the hate disturbed and

saddened him, but Mikala's comment pushed anger to the forefront. Goddamn it, why couldn't they leave her alone? He took a screen shot of the comments and sent it to Irisa. Then, he deleted the post and changed the settings so no one but him could post or share anything.

But that didn't seem like enough. He wanted to throttle each and every person who'd hurt her.

He needed to hit something. But more than that, he needed to hold her.

He closed the computer and went in search of her.

Two weeks to go until Jett's show. Hopefully things would calm down by the time they landed in New York. Until then, he intended to make their time in California the best two weeks of Audrey's life.

In between working with Hugh and overseeing Wild Intentions practice sessions, Luke did his best to convince Audrey that life in California was better than life in New York, packing their days with wine tasting at vineyards, hiking, shopping, an undersea boat tour, lots of time on the beach, and lots of time in his bed.

She kept remarking about all the extra space in his house, the size of the rooms, the amount of natural light. And he kept picturing different scenarios where she'd want to stay permanently.

She fit perfectly in his life, whether they were working on the set design for Wild Intention's performance on Jett's show, or she was accompanying him to practice sessions at Zander's house, or they were spending time with his band mates. Jayne and Irisa remarked on how much they liked having her there, too. And Luke knew he'd never tire of seeing her in his bed or sharing morning coffee or glasses of wine in the evening on the bedroom balcony.

Pride had shot through him when he'd accompanied her to meet with the regional director of the anti-bullying program. He'd held her hand while she told her story and asked the director how she could help others. They'd left the meeting with a commitment for Audrey and Luke to sign on as celebrity ambassadors, and a promise from Audrey to donate proceeds of special, anti-bullying designs to the program.

He knew he was sunk when he brought her to see the community center where he and the other guys would be spending the next few months volunteering their time teaching music to kids. She charmed the kids there, and he could see her getting involved there, too.

The last morning of their stay in L.A., he found her in the lower level of his home, sketchbook in hand, staring out the patio window. "You okay?"

"Sure." She set her sketchbook aside and rose to wrap her arms around his waist. "I'm just working on design ideas for the anti-bullying campaign."

He kissed the top of her head. "You know, this space down here would make a good studio for you."

She tilted her head and gazed around the room and then smiled. "It is a great space."

Her answer was more noncommittal that he wanted to hear, but he didn't want to push her too hard.

She still had some time left on her lease. He'd use their time in New York to continue convincing her that L.A.—and with him—was where she needed to be.

CHAPTER THIRTEEN

On Tuesday morning, her first full day back in the city, Audrey sat with Luke on the couch in her apartment, finishing up her second cup of coffee. They had two days to themselves until the rest of The Fury and Wild Intention would arrive to select clothes for their performance on Jett's show that Friday.

Her cell phone rang and the studio property manager's number lit across her screen. Her lease renewal would be coming up soon. Maybe he wanted to talk about it. She set her cup aside and engaged the call. "Hi, Mauro."

"The front of your studio has been vandalized, with graffiti all over the windows. I have the police here. They'd like to talk to you. Can you come in now? I called Renee, she's on her way."

Dread weighted her stomach and she clutched the phone tight. "What the hell? Are you serious? I'll be there in ten minutes."

"What's wrong?" Luke asked from behind her.

Focused, she didn't answer, just tossed her phone in her purse and dashed to the bathroom to brush her teeth. She'd been a fool. What made her think that not checking the internet meant the fans had given up?

"What's going on?" Luke grabbed her toothbrush wrist.

She spit into the sink and wiped her mouth with the back of her other hand. The words gushed out on a half sob. "Graffiti on the studio. The police," she swallowed hard. "The police are there and want to talk to me."

A dark expression covered his face. "I'm coming with you."

Minutes later, the cab screeched to a stop behind the police car.

Audrey looked out the window and her breakfast threatened to make a reappearance.

Ugly words, sprayed across the windows, in huge bright red letters. The giant words would be visible from a block away. Her surroundings began to spin. She squeezed her eyes shut to block out the words, but they were just as big and bright behind her eyelids.

Slut. User. Whore. Die Bitch!

Tears stung her eyes and rolled down her hot cheeks. How much more could she take? They'd threatened her life for chrissake.

Luke gripped her hand and guided her out of the cab toward Mauro, Renee, and the police officer. She was only too glad when the cop suggested they go inside.

The officer introduced herself, but Audrey missed the name thanks to the buzzing in her ears. She made herself focus while the woman kept talking.

"Ma'am, do you have any idea who could have done this?"

Her thoughts ran to Mikala. Luke's super fan was local and hated her. But in reality, Luke had millions of fans. She told her about Mikala and the nasty internet postings on her site and finished up with the truth. "It could be anyone."

With an expression promising murder, Luke rattled off his own brief summary of the cyberattacks.

The officer nodded, jotted down notes, and asked Mauro a few questions more before leaving. "I'll be in touch."

Mauro scrubbed his hands over his face. "I'll get someone out here to scrape the paint off the window. It may take a few days, but hopefully not more than that. And I'll have it covered up with cardboard while it's being worked on. I'll call you as soon as it's set up. Cardboard will go up today."

Audrey held herself together. When Mauro left, she went to her office in the back room. Who would do this? The letters were shaky, not straight, but that gave them more of a horror movie vibe. Had that been deliberate?

Luke pushed open the door. His eyes burned with anger. "Come on, let's get out of here."

"No. I need to work. I was going to come in to do the books today and that's what I'm going to do. Business as usual." Her fingers shook. She folded her arms across her chest to hide her trembling hands.

"Fine. I'm grabbing coffee from the shop down the street, I have a phone call to make and then I have an errand to run. I'll meet you back here." He pressed a kiss to her forehead and strode away.

She watched him go until he disappeared into the coffee shop. "He's in a dark mood."

"Well, I can understand why." Renee held the door for her.

Audrey's fingers continued to shake while she did the books, and while Renee and she prepared for their conference call with Frozen Blur's manager. The new all-woman rock band had apparently loved her designs from the show.

When the band's manager came through on video chat, she had the entire band with her. "We want everything from the runway show."

"Excuse me?" Audrey spanned the six women in the screen.

"The metallic pieces, the leather, the spandex, the chains. All of it. Except the menswear, of course."

The woman sitting to the manager's right, with pale pink hair and a diamond nose piercing gave her a wave. "Your name is all over the place right now. People love to hate you, and we love stirring up trouble, so of course, we need your designs."

The *love to hate you* line bothered her. "Um, thank you?"

"But mainly we love the designs anyway and want to book you for our album photo shoot next month."

"I would love that. I'm very excited to work with you." Audrey kept her voice professional but couldn't control the huge smile spreading across her face. After such a shitty, scary morning, and all the petty online bullshit, she really needed some good news.

As she pulled up her calendar and talked with the manager about available dates, Renee gave her a big grin off camera. After the call ended, Audrey glanced at her own hands. Apparently, an ounce of kindness and a huge sale were a good cure for trembling.

Luke arrived a while later. "Here you are, iced coffee and a whistle to add to your keyring." He set them on her desk, then turned and gave Renee the same.

"What's with the whistle?" She tried it out and the shrill sound blasted Audrey's ears so much she jumped. Then Renee giggled, "Never mind, I figured out what it's for."

He stayed in the background while she finished the books. Close, but not in the way. After that, the stress of the morning caught up with her and her concentration was fried. She sent Renee home and closed up early.

Luke convinced her to see a movie. They sat in the last row of a darkened, nearly empty theater, with a bucket of popcorn between them, watching a comedy that didn't require heavy concentration. Laughing helped ease the hollow feeling in her soul.

They picked up dinner from the sushi place close to her apartment. And then finally, they were home.

Luke set the food on plates and she opened a bottle of white wine. They hadn't talked about it, and she needed to. Someone coming after her in one of her personal spaces scared her. "Who do you think did it?"

"Your guess is as good as mine. The obvious

choice would be Mikala. I spent a long time today looking through the most frequent commenter profiles for clues. No luck. That's when I picked up the whistles. It's not much of anything, but it made me feel better."

"I appreciate all the support you gave me today." She rose onto her toes, until she could reach his lips, and kissed him.

He drew her into the living room and nudged her until she sat on the edge of the couch. He sat behind her, legs splayed on either side of hers, and massaged the tension from her shoulders. Over and over, he worked the muscles in her back, shoulders, neck, and head, varying pressure and speed. She sipped wine and everything mellowed.

He kissed her between her shoulder blades and started singing, his voice low, more of a whisper against her skin, and he kept it up as he melted the stress from her body. That same song he'd been singing since the first night he'd stayed over. The song was older than she was, had been written before she was born, but when he sang it, she thought of it as only hers.

She settled against him. "I'm glad you're here."

"Sunshine, I'll always be here."

That wouldn't be the case. Eventually, he'd want to go back home to California. Eventually, the band would start recording, and then touring, and getting increasingly busy with Furious Records. And then she wouldn't be able to rely on him to calm her down or make things better, or have him to hold every night.

She needed to start getting used to handling

things on her own. Too soon, he'd be out of her life.

CHAPTER FOURTEEN

Audrey had been awake for hours by the time the alarm clock pealed, signaling the start to another new day. Sleep had come in small doses while her thoughts had run rampant, darting from clothes choices for the bands, to the slurs on her windows, to the sexy, solid man sleeping beside her.

She hit the off button and rolled out of bed.

"Too early," Luke murmured from beneath the covers. "We're still on California time."

Her lips twitched. She wished they were still in California. Things seemed happier for her out there. "You can sleep in if you want. I have to go to work."

He sat up reaching for her. "I think it's better if you wait until the spray paint is gone before you go in."

"As hurtful as it is, I can't let it stop me. I need to reorganize some things." She pressed a kiss to his hand. "Go back to sleep. Maybe you can meet me later for lunch."

"No, I'll go in with you. I have a few calls to make anyway." He tossed the covers aside and rose. "I'll give you space and hang out at the coffee shop. Then do my own thing until lunch, when I'm going to convince you to play hooky for the rest of the day."

"Think so, huh?"

"Don't underestimate my powers of persuasion." Strong hands clamped on her waist and dragged her against him.

She wrapped her arms around him and enjoyed the feeling of solid male still warm from sleep. "I like your persuasive powers."

"Enough to climb back in bed? The sheets are still warm."

Nipping his lip, she laughed. How was he always able to make her forget about the bad things? "Let me make a dent in my to-do list at the studio. That way, if I play hooky later, I won't feel too guilty. Everyone is coming in tomorrow to select clothes for Friday's show. I want to be ready."

"That reminds me, I have a radio interview at three o'clock today with the local rock station to promote Friday's show. An in-station interview for an hour, taking calls and discussing the new band."

"Better set an alert in your phone. I don't want to be responsible for you missing it."

When she stepped out of the cab half an hour later with Luke, the ugly slurs hidden behind large sheets of cardboard taunted her. She tightened her hand in his.

"You don't have to go in today." He rubbed her back with his other hand. "Putting off the organizing for a few days won't hurt anything."

"No. I'm going in." She unlocked the door, surprised when Luke followed her inside. "I thought you were going to the coffee shop."

"I am. When Renee gets here."

"I'll be fine on my own." But she was glad he was staying.

When Renee breezed in twenty minutes later, he kissed Audrey goodbye. "I'll be back at noon."

She locked the door behind him and glared at the red paint covered by cardboard obscuring her view of the street. Pretending to be fine hadn't worked. Luke had seen through her ruse. She hadn't told him the organizing was a start for packing up the studio.

Renee stood at her desk, checklist in hand. "What's up with the list?"

"My lease is up in a few months. I'm not renewing here."

"I don't blame you. That graffiti is bad energy. Where are you thinking of moving the studio?"

"I'm not sure yet. But it's time to start looking."

"I'll keep my eyes and ears open." Renee settled onto the floor two feet from her empty chair and sipped her tea. Audrey had given up trying to figure out Renee's quirks.

"Do me a favor? Don't mention anything to Luke. I don't want him to think I'm spooked about the spray painter."

"But you are spooked."

"But I don't want him to worry."

"Got it. We're totally cool. Unflappable women just checking out some new digs."

Laughing felt good. "Yes, we are. If you don't mind, I want to double-check the inventory to make it easier to estimate the number of moving boxes and the moving truck size we'll need."

They worked side by side, not stopping for a

break until the mail arrived at eleven-thirty. Audrey dusted her hands on her pants and dropped the letters onto her desk. She'd also received a large package.

Renee pointed at the box. "What did you order? Anything fun?"

"I'm not waiting on anything. I have no idea what this is." She turned it over, seeking the return address. No name, just a New York City street she didn't recognize. She grabbed a box cutter and sliced across the top and then dug through a layer of newspaper. She instantly recognized the material and pattern of one of her designs. Frowning, she pulled out the fabric. The bronze dress sprinkled with sequins was identical to the one she'd worn to the fashion show. It had been one of her best-selling pieces from the Fall collection.

It was in tatters.

Her breath caught. Large, ugly gashes crisscrossed the chest and back of the dress. Dried drips of brownish red were splattered all over it...

Like blood.

Icy cold shot up her spine.

A single sheet of paper lay at the bottom of the box. She reached for it with tingling hands. She didn't want to read it. Didn't want to know. But she couldn't look away.

Stay away from Luke or next time this will be YOU.

"What's wrong, Aud? You've gone white." Renee's voice came from far away.

Spots appeared in front of her eyes. Audrey's heart pounded as fast as a needle whipping through a straight seam.

"Oh, shit." Renee took the dress from her hands and eased her into a chair. "Deep breaths and put your head between your knees. I'll call the police."

She nodded, or gave some semblance of a nod.

Numbness overtook her body.

The hate would never stop.

She couldn't handle it anymore.

***

Luke spent the morning on the phone with the contractor who'd renovated Irisa and Dom's house. Halfway into the lengthy chat, he'd realized having Audrey in on the call would have helped immensely. Still, he received an estimate on how long it would take to convert the lowest level of his home into usable studio space for Audrey. He'd wanted her there anyway, but the vandalism had pushed him to get the project done immediately.

Then he called Irisa and Zander to report in on Audrey. In painstaking detail, he told them what had been happening. Sweat beaded all over his face while Zander insisted they think about getting Audrey a security guard and Irisa exclaimed her relief about the authorities now being involved. He felt like he needed another shower. More importantly he needed to figure out who was behind the spray paint. Close to noon, he ended the call and then walked back to the studio.

From down the block he saw two cops walk through the previously locked door. Fear choked his heart and he ran hard, flinging back the door and taking the stairs two at a time. He knew he shouldn't have left her alone. Not even with Renee. He burst inside the studio, screaming her name. "Audrey?"

Four pairs of eyes turned toward him—two cops, Renee, and his precious Audrey, pale and shaking.

He moved to her as fast as he could. "What's going on? Why are the cops here, again?"

Audrey pointed to a tattered bloody dress in one of the officer's gloved hands. "I had a special delivery. A stay-away-from-Luke-special."

The one cop showed him a sheet of paper. "This note was found in the box."

Stay away from Luke or next time this will be YOU.

Fuck. "What can you do with this?"

The first cop answered. "The only identifying information they used is two crumpled pieces of newspaper from last Sunday's circulation. The return address is a fake. Ms. Pierce gave us a list of the clients who ordered that dress. We'll go through the list, but considering the dress has been available on the secondary market, that's not a lot to go on. We'll test everything for prints, but if there's nothing in the system, there's nothing we can do."

"What about the blood?"

"That could be anything too. We're not sure this is real blood but we'll have it tested."

"The message was clear enough." Audrey's hands shook and her body trembled. She rocked back and forth.

Luke wrapped his arms around her. "We had an incident yesterday with the spray paint on the front window. The property manager called it in."

"Yeah," the second cop nodded. "But we'll need the three of you to come down to the station to give statements."

Luke nodded. "Whatever you need."

Two hours later, after enduring another retelling of the cyberattacks and watching Audrey's shaking slow to a stop and cool stillness set in, Luke accompanied Audrey and Renee from the police station and back to the studio. Renee found work in the front room, leaving him alone with Audrey in her office. This had gone way too far. Anger and fear mixed together into a dangerous cocktail. Luke pulled her into his embrace. "Nothing's going to happen to you. I promise."

"How? How exactly can you promise that?" Her voice rose octaves higher. "Things keep getting worse, not better."

"I can help." He held her tighter. "It's okay. We'll fix this."

"It's not okay. And you can't fix this." She wrenched free. "Every time I post a picture online, I'm being attacked. My name is dragged through the mud every day. It's hurting my livelihood and it's killing me inside. I thought I could handle that part, but this..." She gestured to her studio window. "This is it. They win. I'm spooked."

"Audrey—"

"That bloody dress? I don't need some rabid fan gutting me because she thinks you're her true love."

"That's not going to happen."

"Really, how can you prove it?"

"We can hire a security guard and get you a

guard dog."

"No. That's no way to live. I love you, Luke, but I'm not going to wait around to see which type of kitchen knife they use to fillet me." She laughed. A bitter, desperate sound. "It's over. They've won. I'll fulfill my obligation to you and the band for the show, but our relationship is over."

Desperation clawed at him. He grasped her hand. "Don't do this. I'm here with you. *With* you. Like I promised."

"I absolve you of your promises. Go back to California, back to your beach, back to your fans. What I said all those weeks ago is true—we don't always get what we want." Tears shimmered, turning blue eyes into pools. She pulled her hand free from his and swiped underneath her eyes. "I'll miss you. I'm glad we gave it a try. But I can't live in constant fear for my life."

His own eyes grew damp—something that hadn't happened in more years that he could remember. He closed his eyes and pinched the bridge of his nose. She'd said she loved him. *Loved* him. And she wouldn't stay. Couldn't stay. How could he let her go?

He opened his eyes and grabbed her by the arms.

She pulled away. "Give me a minute. I'm going to the restroom."

His phone rang. *What now?* He glanced at the screen and swore. The fucking radio interview. "Hello?"

"Hi, Mr. Thompson. I'm checking on your estimated arrival time. The show is live in twenty minutes."

Goddamn. Fucking. Hell. "I'm on my way."

He backtracked to the front room and found Renee. "Tell Audrey I had to go. I forgot about the radio interview. Tell her we're not finished with our conversation. I'll be back as soon as I can."

"No problem. I'll take care of her until you're back." Her smile indicated she hadn't heard any part of his conversation with Audrey.

He ran for a cab, intent on finding a way to cut the interview short.

By the time he returned to the studio, an hour and a half later, it was locked. Audrey and Renee had gone.

Anger and fear twisted into one again. She was probably at home. No need to panic.

As soon as he set foot in her place, he knew she'd been there. Her perfume hung heavier in the air.

His suitcases were stacked on the floor in front of the couch, close to the door, far from their place in the bedroom. Seeing them there was like a sucker punch to his stomach. On top, lay a note in her flowing script.

Luke,

I'm staying with Renee tonight. I wasn't sure how late you'd get in from your interview, so you can sleep at my place, but please move your things to a hotel tomorrow morning. If you need clothes for Friday's show, I'll see you at the studio tomorrow at noon for the bands' appointment. Regardless, please drop my key in my mailbox after you lock up in the morning.

It was signed simply *Audrey.*

Goddamn it. He slammed his fist onto the dresser.

He dialed her number and cursed the automated voice mail recording. "Audrey. I know you're upset, but we can figure this out." He closed his eyes, suddenly weary and discouraged. "I love you. I need you. Just call me and come home."

Three hours after he'd left the message, Audrey still hadn't returned his call or returned home. He should leave and find a hotel but on the off chance she came back, he wasn't missing an opportunity to talk to her.

He paced the apartment, alternating between hating and loving each item that reminded him of her. Hopes crushed and royally pissed off, he initiated a video chat with the band.

One by one, they picked up, until he had Irisa, Jayne, Zander, Brendan, and Landry on his screen.

He didn't wait to exchange greetings. "Audrey received a serious threat today." He launched into the story, cringing and angry all over again. When he'd finished, everyone was silent.

He shoved a hand through his hand and forced himself to focus. "So, I don't know what to do. She's scared out of her mind that someone is going to kill her."

"Luke," Jayne's soft voice spoke up. "Hold it together. Channel that anger. Use it to focus on a solution."

"I'm trying to think of one. My posting a please be nice message didn't do a damn bit of good."

"Then do the one thing I'm always cautioning

against—go on a tirade." Irisa nodded at him when he frowned. "You need to get as much attention as possible and reach as many people as possible, and you exploding might finally get those commenting to shape up."

He let the idea settle. Tirade—he could do a tirade. Like they'd never believe. "Jett's show is live. I can ask him for two minutes of air time at the end of the show, after we perform with Wild Intention."

"That's smart, man. I'm sure he'd let you do it." Zander gave him a thumbs up.

"Hold up." Jayne waved at the screen. "Owen and Swindle Ox just released an announcement. They're going to be on Jett's show with us. A last-minute fill in for Jon Briarline. Jon's wife went into early labor and he's staying in Seattle to be with her. Swindle Ox is in the city this week, performing some private shows."

Goddamn Owen. Shit. "It doesn't matter. We're still going to do what we need to do."

"Don't forget, you'll have us with you. We always have your back." Zander met his gaze. "Try to get some sleep. We'll all see you in the morning."

A phone call to Jett secured his two minutes of air time at the end of the show. After texting the confirmation to Zander, he asked Jayne and Irisa to check in on Audrey.

The bottle of whiskey on the top shelf of Audrey's cabinet had his name on it.

Despair set in, and being surrounded by her things made his feelings all that much harder to explain.

Ignoring his social media sweep, ignoring everything else, he poured the first shot.

He just wanted to be numb.

Early morning sunlight beamed across Luke's face. He woke up alone, in Audrey's bed. Dull pain throbbed in his temples when he raised his head. She hadn't come back and she hadn't called. He'd woken up countless times during the night to check.

His phone, on her pillow, blinked with missed messages from Zander and Irisa. She'd sent him the band's hotel information, along with a room reservation for himself. He took his time getting ready to leave, wondering if this were the last time he'd ever be in Audrey's space.

When he reached her mailbox, he paused, bags at his side, turning the key over and over in his hand. To him, dropping it in said giving up on them. But, keeping it said he couldn't follow her wishes.

He stood for a long time before finally making his decision.

CHAPTER FIFTEEN

After a night spent tossing and turning on a futon in Renee's apartment, Audrey unlocked her studio at eleven-thirty, intending to stay open only for the appointment with the bands. Safety had been shattered with the dress delivery. Whoever had sent it knew where she was and that made her a sitting target. She and Renee hustled inside and then she locked the door behind her.

Renee set her tea on the table. "Are you sure you don't want me to handle this appointment on my own?"

"I made a commitment. I'm seeing it through." Though it would be hard. Really hard. Especially when she saw Luke.

In his emotional message, he'd said he loved her. *Loved* her. But fear kept her from celebrating that love and creating a life with him. She loved him and he loved her, but someone else wanted him enough to try to blot her out of existence.

"Do me a favor?" She waited for Renee to catch her gaze. "Do whatever you have to do to keep this appointment rolling."

"We need to be out of here at two o'clock to meet with the real estate agent anyway."

Mauro had been understanding about her

decision to not renew her lease. "Let's try for one-thirty and I'll buy you lunch."

"If it's going to be a repeat of last night's dinner and breakfast this morning where I ate and you picked at your food and pretended, I'll pass. That was depressing. You need to eat."

Audrey pretended she hadn't heard that remark. "Mauro's brother and his construction crew will be here in a bit to scrape the paint off the windows. It will be nice to have sunlight coming in again."

"So, we'll have a full house with the bands in here and those guys out there."

"I'm hoping for a combination of chaos and a circus." Enough distractions to keep her mind off Luke and off seeing that mutilated dress in her mind.

A short while later, she received her wish.

Wild Intention arrived first. Hugh, Chelsea, Autumn, and Spike wandered in, talking over each other, and pointing out clothes. Audrey immediately began working with the guys and let Renee handle the girls. While she helped Spike try on different jackets, Mauro's brother arrived with his crew and set up outside.

Fifteen minutes later, The Fury trooped in. The space filled up fast with eight rockers, plus Jayne and Irisa.

Audrey met Luke's gaze. He stared at her with so much emotion that her own eyes stung with tears she refused to shed. She let Landry catch her attention and turned away from Luke.

Behind her, Renee spoke to him, asking his opinion on something for Hugh. The nervous new singer relied on Luke's opinion for everything. Thank goodness for Hugh. Audrey moved from person to person, ignoring the unspoken questions in Irisa and Jayne's expressions.

A few people from Mauro's brother's crew came inside to meet the band. In the corner of her vision, Luke shook hands with one of the guys and then stepped outside to talk to another. Curiosity piqued, she strained to listen but was too far away to hear. Was he talking about the vandalism or something as simple and happy as a past concert?

Brendan cleared his throat, startling her. "Hey. Audrey?"

She forced a smile onto her cheeks. "Sorry. I'm a little distracted. Did you want to see a different shirt? I have more of the organic cotton you like in the back."

"We're all sorry about what happened yesterday. That's pretty scary."

"Thank you."

He leaned in. "Talk to Luke."

She couldn't have this conversation. Not when emotions were so close to the surface. She patted the soft mossy green shirt he held. "That color will look good on you. If you're all set, I'd better help whoever hasn't made a decision yet."

Before he could answer, she backed away and helped Chelsea make a final decision on a leather dress.

Luke's voice carried to her from a few feet away. He stood arms crossed, in front of Renee. "Audrey always picks my things for me."

"Audrey is busy. I can help you." Hands on her

hips, Renee stared back, looking just as stubborn. Her tiny assistant could be a bulldog when she wanted to be.

Luke narrowed his gaze. "I can wait."

Those three words brought back the image of him standing in her sun-drenched studio the first day he'd arrived with his crazy proposition. Biting the inside of her cheek, Audrey crossed the few steps separating them and pointed out the blue shirt, faded jeans and braided leather bracelet she'd set aside. "How's this?"

"It would be better if you'd talk to me." His fingertips grazed her knuckles as she handed him the clothes.

Goosebumps pebbled on her skin. "We talked yesterday. I agreed to fulfill my promise on this job. Professional is all I can do."

"No. It's not." He leaned in, face earnest, until all she could see was him. "Audrey..."

"Excuse me." Renee stepped in between them and cupped her hands over her mouth, raising her voice to carry over the other conversations in the room. "Guys, it looks like everyone is all set. Audrey and I have an appointment at two o'clock, so we only have a few more minutes here to wrap things up."

Wild Intention crowded between her and Luke, exuding profuse thanks and asking if she'd help them get ready for the show. Renee kept control and had everyone cleared out of the studio in under ten minutes.

Ignoring Luke didn't mean she hadn't been aware of him. She'd felt his gaze as surely as if he'd been caressing her skin and missed it as soon as the door had closed at his back. Silence lay heavy in the absence of the ten voices that had filled the space for the past two hours. Too heavy. She again relied on Renee to distract her from her heartache and tried to psych herself up for the real estate appointment.

Viewing four potential studio spaces made her head spin. Finally, they were through with the showings and she headed home. The hallway mailbox was her first stop. Her spare key lay at the bottom of the otherwise empty box.

Alone.

Just like her.

***

Friday evening, Luke paced the green room at *Hard and Heavy Live*. He needed to talk to Audrey.

She'd arrived with Renee just after he'd come in with the band. They'd made eye contact but hadn't spoken, separated by too many people clambering for their attention. By the time he'd settled his obligations, she and Renee were busy with the show's hair and make-up people, helping Wild Intention get ready. The new band members were still finishing prep and Landry and Brendan had joined them to calm any last-minute nerves.

Zander and Jayne sat on the couch to his left. They'd given up talking to him. He couldn't blame them. He couldn't concentrate on anything but Audrey and the speech he planned to give.

He wasn't worried at all about the performance

itself. He'd spent all day rehearsing with his band and the new kids. Kids. Hell, how jaded was he? He wasn't even ten years older than the youngest one but inside, he felt ancient.

Zander held out his phone. "Stop pacing and check this out—a group of fans from Anaheim have dubbed themselves Audrey's Army. They're going around stomping down the nasty comments fans are leaving on every social media site."

"Seriously?" He grabbed Zander's phone. His final contestant, Nicole, and her sisters Coco, Serena, Desiree, and Olivia were leading the charge. When he got back to L.A., they were definitely going to talk and get something lined up for the sisters.

"I contacted them and expressed our thanks." Jayne smiled, her cheeks growing pink. "Olivia responded back. They're gaining momentum. A lot of people are tired of the mean comments. She's turning this into an anti-bullying campaign."

Finally, some positive news. Maybe the tide was turning. "I'm glad to hear it. I'll make sure I contact her too."

He resumed pacing. The TV mounted on the wall broadcasted the live show. With the sound muted, he watched Owen and his band chat with Jett.

Zander sat with his arm around Jayne's shoulders, threading his fingers through her hair as she scrolled through her phone. "Luke, you're never this keyed up before a concert. Did you talk to Audrey yet?"

"No." He paused in front of the couple. With

every passing second, he felt like he was that much closer to spiraling out of control. He raked his hands through his hair and admitted his greatest fear. "Maybe there's no coming back from this. Maybe she doesn't love me enough. Or maybe this is what I get for all the crap I put you two through."

Jayne tossed her phone onto the cushion, jumped up and hugged him. "Don't even think that. We don't hold it against you. You were hurting back then and you've more than made up for it."

"Don't mention the past again, man. It's forgotten. We're good." Zander hugged him too. "We're rooting for you. You'll get this thing with Audrey fixed."

He didn't deserve friends as good as these guys, but damn, he was lucky he had them.

The door swung open. Wild Intention came in. They were confident. They were ready. Good thing, because they were about to go on.

He glanced behind them, seeking his brunette beauty. "Where's Audrey?"

Landry came in, followed by Brendan. "She left."

He forced a breath through his tightening chest. "What do you mean, she left?"

The bassist shrugged. "She said the clothes were purchased, not on loan, so she didn't need them back. And she had a headache and was going home. Renee went too."

Emptiness enveloped him. Was this how his life would be? Goddamn, it sucked.

A knock rapped on the door. "Five minutes, guys."

Zander motioned for the new band to come together. "Hugh, Chelsea, Autumn, and Spike, break a leg out there. You're going to rock this place. Get the crowd nice and warmed up, and then when we join you, this place will explode."

They gathered for a group high-five and then trooped toward the stage. Luke stayed near Hugh, watching the young singer for signs of nerves. "Want to do some quick breathing exercises?"

Maybe they'd help the ache in his chest.

"Sure." They worked through three sets, until Jett welcomed Wild Intention and the newly formed band got ready at the instruments on the left of the set.

Brendan dropped his hand onto Luke's shoulder. "I don't know about you guys, but I feel like a proud teacher now. They've been working so hard."

Luke grunted his agreement. He wanted Hugh to do well. The kid's performance would be a reflection on him and the band's performance would be a reflection on The Fury.

The set lights dimmed. Lights flashed in the background, highlighting the logo Audrey had designed. Drums broke out with a pounding beat. A heavy guitar riff followed. And Hugh launched into *Lights Out*.

They rocked the song. Fucking rocked it. Around him, the guys were grinning and exchanging high-fives.

Luke smiled, nodding his head to the beat. Pride for them warmed the empty void within. He continued his breathing exercises, waiting for The

Fury's cue to join in.

The audience roared when his band walked on set. Just as they'd practiced, Wild Intention jumped into *Cut Down*, and the bands played together. As he sang with Hugh, Luke let the music take him. It had been his first love. Maybe it would be all that he had left.

Applause rolled over him like thunder. Loud and long and deafening. Breathing hard, he hugged Hugh and congratulated the bands on a job well done.

As the cheers slowed, Jett joined them, waving his arms for quiet. "As I mentioned at the start of the show, Luke has a special announcement he'd like to make. Luke, take it away, buddy."

Jett and Wild Intention moved off to the side. Luke grabbed hold of the mic again. At the corner of his vision, Brendan, Zander, and Landry moved in closer, forming a solid unit of support at his back.

He'd been planning his tirade to smash the haters into silence. But standing there, his heart swelled. He stared into the camera. "I've been in a relationship with Audrey Pierce for a while. But fan comments on our relationship and especially on her as a person are tearing her, and us, apart. You've ignored my requests to stop the comments. I've always been grateful for my fans, but not when you try to steal my life. And that's what you're doing. You deem yourselves judge, jury, and executioner on a situation you know nothing about."

He paused and felt the support pouring in from his band behind him and Jayne and Irisa at the side of the set. "You've made me what I am. But now, you're ruining the best thing that's ever happened to me. And for the first time in my life, it's made me resent you. Someone recently sent Audrey a direct threat on her life. That's going too far. All of this is going too far. It needs to stop—now. I don't want the kind of fans who want to kill my happiness. You don't know what's best for me. I do. I love Audrey and I'm not letting her go. If you can't deal with that, then I suggest you stop following me on all platforms. Because if I ever meet one of the fuckers who made her doubt herself or our relationship, they're going to feel the full brunt of The Fury."

Jett crossed to him and touched his arm. "Luke, do you have anything you want to say directly to Audrey, in case she's listening?"

He must have learned that Audrey had left. Luke checked his emotions. "Yeah." He cleared his throat and took a breath, and then began singing the old love song he now thought of as Audrey's song. Hopefully, wherever she was, she was watching.

When he finished, he looked straight into the camera and imagined staring into Audrey's captivating eyes. "I'm not letting go, Audrey. We need each other. Come back to me."

Waves of applause washed over him. The show ended, and Jett clapped him on the back.

He'd done all he could do.

Luke headed backstage while the rest of the band chatted with Jett. When he reached the hallway, Owen waited by the green room. "I can't believe they cut three minutes of my band's air time for that drivel."

Luke raised an eyebrow at him and walked

past. He finally saw Owen for what he was—petty and pathetic and not worth his time.

"What, no comment?" Owen followed him. "You pussy. A little red paint on an old dress and window is enough to send you and your little woman into a tailspin?"

The words sunk in fast. The damaged dress hadn't hit the news. Anger flowed faster than lava. Luke whipped around ready to rage at Owen. "What the fuck? You sent the dress? You did the spray paint?"

Owen smirked and raised his chin a little higher. "Consider it payback for embarrassing me at the launch party. Pretty good prank, huh?"

In the span of a second, Luke had Owen pressed up against the wall. "You brought that fucking embarrassment upon yourself. That doesn't justify what you did to my girlfriend. You fucking scared her. That isn't a prank. That was way beyond a fucking prank."

Owen fought against the hold. "Messing with you is too easy. Those girls posting all the hater comments gave me the idea. And the way you've been acting over her... I figured I'd mess with Audrey because she's such a touchy subject with you."

All the fury he'd tamped down for the sake of Audrey busted free of his worn out control. Luke grabbed Owen by the throat and slammed the back of his head against the wall so hard it left a dent. "I could put you in the hospital for six months. But unlike you, I'm not a sadistic asshole. You hate me. I hate you. But I never extended that hatred to your family or friends. You're going to jail, fuck-face."

"Whatever." Owen pushed him off by shoving his hands into Luke's chest.

Luke's reflexes were faster than ever. He landed a right cross squarely into Owen's jaw. The singer stumbled backward and slumped down. Luke went after him, ready to pound him into the concrete floor.

"You got in a solid shot, now rein it in." Landry's Texas drawl pulled him back to the reality of his surroundings.

He loomed over Owen, boot resting on his stomach, but kept his fists to himself. "You fucking bastard. You went too far. She thought someone was deranged enough to try to kill her."

Vanessa stepped into his view. "Owen? Is this true? You did those things to Audrey?"

Zander pulled Luke away. "Let's go. We're done here."

"I can't let him get away with this."

"He won't. We all heard him." Face grim, Zander jerked his thumb over his shoulder, indicating his band mates, Jett, studio employees, Wild Intention, and members of Swindle Ox.

Vanessa stalked to Owen, still on the floor. "What were you thinking? Do you know how many shows I've been in with her? How much she's supported me? You worked with her too. And you'd do this to her?"

Owen opened his mouth to speak, but she rolled right over him. "You're going to apologize. Publicly. Or we're through. Hell, we're through anyway. But you're still going to apologize for this and accept responsibility."

Jayne's hand on his arm drew Luke's attention away from the arguing couple. "Audrey needs you. You have to go to her. We'll handle this. Go get your girl."

He walked away from Owen. Getting to Audrey, getting her to listen, mattered more than anything else.

CHAPTER SIXTEEN

In the quiet of her apartment, Audrey lay across the bed watching the video clip Jayne had sent her. Luke's impassioned plea brought tears to her eyes. His song caused the tears to fall fast.

As sweet and heartfelt and moving as it was, it might not do any good. He couldn't control the fans, and whoever had sent her the sliced dress was still out there somewhere. Reasoning didn't work with some people.

She rolled onto her back and watched the video again. She missed him. Had she made a mistake in ending things? Fear had pushed in, demanding she break off all ties. As badly as her heart ached, Luke's probably hurt just the same. She was making them both miserable because she didn't want to spend her life worrying about crazy fans, or bodily harm, or targeted attacks.

Being alone meant no drama but also no love. The ache in her soul intensified.

She pushed off the bed and stared out at the romantic view of the city at sunset. Glittering lights dotted buildings against streaks of pink and orange.

Along with her design space, her apartment lease would be up soon. Maybe finding new digs for both places, far away from everyone and everything familiar, would be smart. Maybe something in a gated community that would keep away knife-wielding maniacs.

Her gut said New York wasn't the right spot anymore.

L.A. felt right.

She pushed that idea from her mind. L.A. would be too close to Luke. She couldn't do that to herself. No matter how much she liked Irisa and Jayne. No matter how happy she'd been there.

Happy.

Luke made her happy. Why wasn't she taking the risk? Being with him, no matter how long they had together, was better than not being with him at all, and was better than this constant ache in her soul. She felt like half of her heart was missing.

The guys had security guards when they needed them. Would life be so bad with one around full time? Didn't she owe it to Luke and to herself to at least try?

A knock sounded at the door.

Rubbing her arms, she crossed her small apartment and peered through the peephole.

Luke stood on the other side of the door. He knocked again. "Audrey, I know you're in there."

Tears pierced her eyes and her heartbeat galloped, pushing her to go to him. This was her chance. She flipped the locks and flung the door open. "Hi."

He looked worn out, exhausted, but his eyes sparked with fire. "I need to talk to you."

"I do, too." She stepped back for for him to pass.

"Let me go first." He stood in the center of the living room, so big and so right in her space. "Owen was the one who sent the dress and did the spray paint."

The shock was overwhelming. Vanessa's attentive boyfriend hadn't seemed capable of such deeds, but then again, he'd done some pretty bad things to Luke over the years. "Are you serious? But why? How did you find out?"

"He did it to get back at me." His features tightened into an angry mask. "Fucking bastard went too far. He actually bragged to me after the show tonight." Unconsciously, he rolled his wrist and she noticed the swollen knuckles.

This time she wasn't upset Luke had taken matters into his own hands. He'd defended her. But hadn't he been doing that all along? Her knees wanted to give out. Part from relief knowing her stalker was done, and part for Luke's terrible turmoil. "I... I don't know what to say."

"I do. Come back to me. I know some of the fans aren't happy about our relationship, but I'm hoping that what I said on the air tonight will help. Also you've recently gotten a fan club of your own. Look." He held out his phone and she read down the screen.

A group called Audrey's Army had set up a site to shame the haters, comment by comment. "They're defending me."

"The girls we met in L.A. started this for you. Lots more have joined in. Most of our fans are cool, and now they're coming out of the woodwork to lend their support."

"Wow." She swallowed hard to fight back tears.

"That's not all." He brought up Owen's personal web page. A public apology to her filled his screen. "Our fans are sharing it, and a few of the rock news sites are carrying it, too. That asshole's already getting a lot of heat for what he did. And, just so you know, I held my temper when I found out. Sort of. After what he put you—put us—through, I had to get in at least one punch."

"Luke." She reached for him, then dropped her hands to her sides. "I'm sorry I got so scared."

He slipped his phone into his pocket. "There's nothing wrong with being scared. It was a scary situation."

She moved closer, needing to feel his heat, his presence, his solid and steady support. "I want to try again. I love you. I realized that nothing is guaranteed. I don't want to give you up because of something that might happen. I'd rather enjoy every single day that we do have together, however long that will be."

"Sunshine." His eyes closed for a moment. When they opened, they were shiny. He gripped her hands. "I love you. I'll take every single day, too."

He tugged her toward him. His arms banded around her and his hands tangled in her hair. Holding tight, she tucked her face into his chest and breathed him in. She had him back and she was never letting go. They stayed wrapped together for a long moment.

Luke eased back enough to trail his roughened fingers over the outline of her face. "I can't wait to get you home."

She nodded. "Home. As in Hermosa Beach?"

"Absolutely. And here I was thinking I'd have to convince you to move your operation to the west coast."

"We can look for a studio."

"Already found a great space, and it's a sweet commute." He slid his hand into her hair again. "My place. The entire bottom level is yours. The contractor can meet with us whenever you're ready."

Excitement spun through her happiness, making her giddy. She peppered his beard with kisses. "I can't believe you did that for me."

"The idea came to me every time I saw you there. It would be perfect for your studio. I want you to be happy."

"You make me happy."

He drew away even further and reached into his pocket and then held out a ring. "And you make me complete."

Her heartbeat pounded and her knees weakened. The pink heart-shaped diamond set in rose gold was delicate, elegant, and perfect. "Luke, it's beautiful."

"I bought this while we were in California. Remember the day when I went to the music store with the guys while you went shopping with Irisa and Jayne? Well, this was the real destination. I was going to wait until the anniversary of the first day we met to propose, but tonight seems like the perfect time." He grasped her left hand. "The first time I saw you, something clicked inside me, like the entire world had suddenly come into focus. Like I'd been waiting for you to complete what was missing in me. Will you marry me and officially become my other half?"

"Yes." She held his gaze while he slipped the ring in place, then she linked their fingers together. "When we met, my heart recognized you as mine. It took the rest of me a little while to catch up, but I want to spend the rest of my life showing you how much I love you."

He lowered his face to hers. Their lips met, sealing their promise of forever.

CHAPTER SEVENTEEN

Luke lounged on his beach chair and stared at the sunlight rippling over the water. He squinted to the horizon where the ocean met the sky. Waves crashing on the shore in the steady ebb and flow pattern soothed him to near sleeping.

Tired. But he couldn't complain because the reason for his lack of sleep was so tempting when curled up around him in bed.

And every time he looked at her, his heart overflowed.

To his left, Zander manned the grill. Somehow, even though they were at Luke's home, Zander had wrangled grill privileges. Luke didn't care too much—the guy knew how to grill. To his right, Landry and Brendan wrestled with Zander and Irisa's dogs in the yard.

The Fury may have been taking a break, but Furious Records had received countless emails and messages from hopefuls and bands needing a new direction. Still, Luke didn't think it would be too long before the guys began making noises about getting back into the studio. Music was in their blood, too strong to ignore.

Twice in the past week, he'd seen Landry scratch new lyrics onto napkins and scraps of paper, and on one occasion, Audrey's sketchbook.

But this time, things would be better. They'd dictate their schedule. They'd make sure all needs were being met. And after all that had happened, they had a better understanding of themselves too.

He was damn lucky for all that he had.

Laughter drifted from the house. The sliding glass door opened, and Irisa, Jayne, and Audrey emerged. Luke met his new fiancée's gaze and grinned. The barbecue to celebrate Audrey's official move to California was underway.

He glanced up to the top level of the house and the master bedroom's balcony. Waking up with Audrey and going to sleep beside her made him alternately grateful and filled with excitement for the future. His other half—his better half—was with him. For good.

Her furniture had arrived the week before and now, little touches of hers wound throughout the house. Mirrors, area rugs, vases, framed pictures, and lots of throw pillows. Instead of *his*, it blended with *hers*, and had become *theirs*. She'd brightened his home the same way she brightened his life.

And every day, he thanked fate for being about to bask in her sunshine.

As their friends celebrated behind them, Audrey slid onto his lap and linked their fingers together. "The girls love my studio."

The renovations to the lower level of the house to match Audrey's design space needs hadn't taken as long as anticipated. She had a warm, inviting, functional space. And plenty of incoming orders to keep both her and Renee busy. Audrey's assistant remained in New York, managing the second location of Audrey Pierce Designs.

Messages of support continued to flow in like a tidal wave, obliterating the negative comments, along with several musicians and fans reaching out to both him and her with their own stories of being bullied. Luke was proud of her for the caring and compassionate way she responded to each message, and for the work she was doing with the anti-bullying program. She'd dressed musicians from every genre for a few of the program's public service announcements and her *Spread Love* t-shirts to benefit the campaign were a nationwide sensation. Luke's love for her gentle, strong spirit grew every day.

"I'm glad you're officially moved in. Now, there's one other thing we need to make official." He rubbed his thumb over the band of her engagement ring.

She kissed his cheek. "I can't wait to marry you. Ready to pick a date?"

"There's only one date I can think of as being perfect for our wedding."

Her smile warmed, brightening the day even more, as she linked her arms around his neck. "The first day we met."

"That's the one." He wrapped his arms around her and brought her even closer until his heart lined up with hers.

They'd come full circle and he couldn't wait to see what life had in store.

"I love you." His heart swelled with how much.

Her hands guided his head down until his lips hovered a breath away from hers. "I love you, too."

Their lips met, soft and warm and perfect together.

As gulls cried overhead and waves crashed on the shore and sparkling sunlight danced over the sea, Luke drew Audrey against his side. True happiness and peace flowed between them.

No matter how long and winding the road had been, he'd finally won Audrey, and that was all that mattered.

LOVE SONG

ABOUT THE AUTHOR

Susan Scott Shelley is an award-winning author of contemporary romance. For as long as she can remember, she has been in love with Love and all the sweeping grand gestures, heart-sighing moments, and quiet comforts it entails.

In addition to writing romances, she is also professional voiceover artist and enjoys lending her voice to a wide range of projects.

An unapologetic optimist, she believes life should be lived with laughter and a sense of wonder. Her favorite things include running, sports, hard rock and old Hollywood movies.

She lives in Philadelphia with her very own Superhero and spends her days writing about tough heroes, smart heroines, and love being the strongest magic there is.

For her newsletter, book information, and more, visit her website: SusanScottShelley.com.